Hearts

Perry E. Zenon

Author

Bedside Books
An imprint of American Book Publishing
P.O. Box 65624 Salt Lake City, UT 84165

www.american-book.com
Printed in the United States of America on acid-free paper.
Hearts
Designed by Designer Name, design@american-book.com

ISBN 1-58982-351-6

Zenon, Perry E., Hearts

Special Sales
These books are available at special discounts for bulk purchases. Special editions, including personalized covers, excerpts of existing books, and corporate imprints, can be created in large quantities for special needs. For more information e-mail info@american-book.com.

Another Day

Dear Lord, I thank You for this,
another day.
Another day to raise You and appreciate
who You are.
I give You the honor
and glory for this,
another day.
Another day to breathe,
to walk,
to do Your will.
Without Your grace,
we would not
have this, another day.
Another day
to hear the birds sing,
to grow in Your World Lord.
I look around me
and I am so
blessed by this, another day.
Another day to seek Your face and
know that You are God.
Today I am filled with joy because You
have given this, another day.

Acknowledgements

To Brenda Green Foucher

For you gave me your all
And expected nothing in return.

Thank You, Rivka Levy

For your patience, understanding
And editorial work of this book.

Sunday

And he did evil,
because he prepared not his heart
to seek the Lord.

2 Chronicles 12:14

Chapter 1

It was very early in the chilly morning. The scene was almost surreal, out of a movie, except to the surly cast of real-time characters. The fog is thick in New Orleans at this time of morning in late May. The heat rises, then cools in the evening and combines with intense moisture from the Mississippi River. If you were standing a short distance from the scene, the prison and convicts would erroneously appear to be embraced in fluffy, sweet, white cotton candy.

A cacophony of dull metal chains erratically clanged together, filling the tightening space as the prisoners unwillingly shuffled into a line to get onto the bus transporting them to a place which, for many of them, would be their home until their spirits would leave their

Hearts

bodies -- the maximum security penitentiary on the remote Louisiana site of Felicia Point.

In addition to the cuffs around their ankles and wrist, another chain connected two inmates together by their ankles to further discourage escape attempts. Each pair was connected by additional serious chain links to those in front and in back of them.

Three transportation marshals stood at the entrance of the bus, checking to make sure that everyone on the incoming roster was accounted for. Two accompanied the detail driver to give passengers their initial indoctrination of prison degradation according to standard procedure, direct the convicts to board.

Their sense of command was greatly enhanced by the newly issued weapons they carried: Kahr K9 Elite compact pistols and DSA SA58 .243 carbines. Enough to stop a busload of convicts.

As the prisoners passed by, the links were separated, leaving only two bound together to enable access to the waiting bus.

"Fill `er up, rear to front."

The prisoners made themselves as comfortable as sardines while the guards entered the bus last, sealing the tomb behind them. While the driver prepared for departure, his associates bellowed the rules, ensuring that they were issued in a way so that even the dumbest passengers understood the rules of compliance.

"You are now inmates of Angola State Penitentiary," the higher-ranking guard screeched as he began to walk down the aisle of the old transport bus that, one wondered, if it could go 130 miles on a good highway.

Perry E. Zenon

"Consider yourselves government property, G.I.s if you will. Here at the pen, you're God's Insults. Get it? G.I.s," he sneered with all the intellect of a man whose ability to get this job was predicated only upon a clean record. Even his high school record was clean--of attendance and interest. He smartly struggled to get his equivalency once he determined he had to earn a living.

"Humph, if it be up to me, all you convicts would be on the first line in Afghanistan; better yet, Iraq," the younger, former military guard interjected as he leaned against the gate separating the passengers from the control area of the bus.

The first one didn't seem to mind the interruption, as if they were an old couple, together so long that they had become accustomed to the other finishing his sentence. Maybe it was because of their similar mentality.

"Might not be able to draft all you at once into our cozy one-man isolation accommodations, but when you screw up, consider yourself volunteering for our isolation militia." The guard chuckled at his cleverness, forgetting that he wasn't even connected with the penitentiary. He was a U.S. Marshall in New Orleans.

"I was just thinking that myself. What a better way to repay your debt to the United States than doin' drive-bys on those we at war wit?"

No response.

The two guards took turns bleating the dos and don'ts and their pet peeves in a sarcastic, scratchy duologue to the uninterested inmates. They were the usual guards on the bus, seemingly relegated forever to this dull job, and they resembled a rehearsed act by a lousy comic duo.

After they were satisfied that the law was laid down and their power had been affirmed, the guards locked the gate and settled in the first seats, in front of the locked, mesh separator, for the trip's duration.

Although talking was amongst the weary list of don'ts, the inmates passed the time with seemingly idle but actually probing chitchat while posturing and scrambling to find a group with whom they would be able to hang and possibly be safe or who their prey would be.

There were those looking for the reassurement of allies in the gangs to which they belonged. One couldn't rely on skin color and their nuances as a guideline to possible or known allies and mortal enemies in such a melting pot of backgrounds as New Orleans was.

Another, also mixed group, diametrically opposed in demeanor, included the religious helpers intending to influence someone else to find God, Allah, Buddha, or any other being who, by their association, would affirm their own worth and power through already personally possessing the "word." Those "insights" were usually left to the hard-timers, discovered during their last time in prison when the reality of expediency set in.

There were always those who were just seeking to not become another man's prison wife; but they were not called homosexual encounters by the participants within the prison's special walls. They were simply exploitations.

Perry E. Zenon

Inmates who were not actively familiar with the term "safety in alliances" were unaware that the guards had duties other than protection once they arrived at their destination.

Midway on the bus sat an inmate shackled to his reverse image. Mitch's self-image, a sharp contrast to the calm, indulged 35ish male, had never remotely included a rise to partnership in an overpriced firm. Mitch Bryant's Black, grossly picturesque body gave the entire message of his life, affiliations, and values. His body was ragingly tattooed as insurance against such a class mistake.

The tattoos depicted a cross on the left side of his neck, a python curling around his right arm from his shoulder to his fist, an intricately stylized acronym for a gang covering his left upper chest with a Cheetah insert. His left bicep once had Satreena imbedded on it. He had to pay extra to superimpose Laquanda over it; both were eight letter words and the capital S was easily converted to L. The latter was the more recent female acquisition. The really lovely kicker was the added, massive, cross-hatched tribal markings.

Twenty-year-old initials and hearts, hand tattooed with ink between his thumb and index finger from reform school days; and what appeared to be two tear drops under his enormous brown eye were culturally suitable to who he was and how Mitch earned his money.

He had not prepared for much of a life on the outside. His adornment would be grounds for immediate disqualification from the military, or an immediate turndown at any interview he would attempt for any blue-collar job with a prestigious employer, such as his pudgy partner.

The CEO to whom he was intimately chained had barely graduated from Harvard (his prestige was as the class anchor-man) and he portrayed a haughtiness to cover up personality failings. Mitch enjoyed his own arrogance at the other end of the social scale.

Mitch's chain-mate was the criminal who seemed to have gotten onto the wrong bus. His clean-shaven, pudgy-faced, well-groomed, non-scarred or tattooed, well-fed good-old-boy, Harvard persona didn't fit in with this crowd of misfits.

Unlike Mitch, who appeared to be the perfect candidate for a prison career, this man just didn't seem to have what it took. He hadn't been a top candidate for the Ivy League school that he had attended through the added allure of family gifts, either. Unlike Mitch, his shackle-mate, he had been endowed to receive the best education attempt that money could buy. He didn't really fit anyplace.

When his company was smaller, he'd been the patronizing type who enjoyed turning down guys like Mitch when they came in for a miserable interview.

His aura of entitlement was surprisingly far from gone, even in these circumstances when characteristics that constituted power in this group were no longer of his real world.

Usually his type could be found on the bus after years of embezzling hundreds of thousands of dollars being tried by the state for his minor infractions before being handed over to the feds.

After detection and sentencing, local embezzlers were often placed into a small cell with two big guys nicknamed Tiny and Zeus. Not too much later, without bought protection, they were destined to become the victim of the ongoing prison wedding march. Sex offenders, particularly of children, weren't so lucky.

Before the criminals even get to the bus from New Orleans to the peninsula on the Mississippi River, the prison-vine usually buzzes with exploitable gossip. Everybody immediately knows who is in the incoming mob scene and that they are either gang relatives or brutal enemies who will be segregated from each other: celebrities, cops gone bad, and those who caught the news media's attention for Louisiana's Most Wanted list.

This inmate, the executive type, astonishingly fell into the latter of the categories.

"Hey, word has it that you killed that little girl."

Mitch was starting a conversation with the person he would spend time with, a stretch longer than the amount of years he had been alive.

"Baby killers don't last too long in this place, too many fathers in here with little girls of their own on the outside," Mitch searched for weakness.

"Come to think about it, the wrong people see me talking to you and I won't even make it through the night!" Mitch, his vocal pitch increasing, was already setting him up for protection extortion, as Mitch was hoping they'd be on the same cell block.

Hearts

"Then don't talk!" Staring out the window, the reject on the bus appeared no more excited about idle chitchat than the average girl is about her first gynecologist visit.

"I don't recall asking you to grace me with your inane conversation," he sneered.

"Hey, man, if I'm goin' to be with you for the rest of my life I might `swell talk to you. Let me ask you question, why you do it, huh?" Mitch's verbal inquiry was punctuated with harsh, hand gang signs, spiky language of an alien culture, as much as the chains would allow.

"I might be a lot of things, but a baby killer I'm not, so if you don't mind, I would like to wrap my mind around something more enjoyable then talking to you," he sniffed.

"Oh, so you're innocent!" Mitch turned a little in his seat toward him, chortling.

"Man, let me tell you somethin' because it might come as a surprise, sweetheart. We's all innocent and we will put that on anyone's grave for them."

"No, I'm guilty--that I am. Don't regret a bit of it. I murdered everyone they convicted me of."

He released a slight snicker and sort of smiled, relishing the attention and astonished admiration. Even the guards surreptitiously leaned backward in their seats to hear.

"Some of my victims they don't even know about. I still remember the first after twelve months and," he said sternly with an air of valor, "neither one of them was a little girl." His word was definitive.

"What, man, you tellin' me? They just said we'd be ridin' with Owens, and how he done that little girl for no reason t'all."

"There is your problem, dog bite. You see the name isn't Owens, it is Mules, Larry Mules." He pronounced his name as though the other guy was a reporter and needed to get it right.

There was a pause while Mitch processed this amazing piece of information.

"Aw dog, you ain't, you ain't that heart person. Louisiana's Most Wanted. Man, I'm sitting next to a real-life serial killer. You killed seventeen women `fore they dinged you. Man, ain't that somethin'."

Mitch proudly informed the occupants of the bus, "I'm chained to a serial killer, whoo-wee!"

The others, most of whom did a double take, quickly passively reposed themselves but weren't shy about staring openly at Mules.

"Twenty." Mules quietly corrected with a sense of controlled theater. In some ways, he was sorry that Louisiana didn't have the drama of executions. He'd go out in a wash of media ink.

"What?" Mitch turned just enough in his seat so that he could really look at Larry Mules. He was slightly thrown off by the unexpected look from the other's cold, blue, somewhat puffy eyes that bored through his own coffee brown eyes.

"Twenty. I murdered twenty people before they caught me, they just couldn't connect the other six to me. Not as smart as they think. I let them know."

Hearts

"Man you kept busy." Mitch finally fell silent as he replayed Mules' statement. After his mental recorder stopped spinning, he looked at Mules as if to comment on his mental stability. On second thought, he contained himself.

"Man, I ain't no math wiz o' nothin' but six and seventeen not twenty, man it's twenty-two."

"You're right, you are no math whiz," Mules meticulously retorted while disgustedly looked out the window again, watching the thick trees pass by as the bus headed down the highway's route to Angola State Maximum Security facility on the isolated penitentiary in Feliciana Parish, 130 miles from the starting point. His mind freely and pleasantly lurched to the spectrum of his extensive criminal career.

"Some of the murders they tried to pin on me were someone else's night of gratification," Mules said absently, but he enjoyed the attention of the famous importance of his status. At least he was finally in an environment that would admire his vicious career--even if he had been exaggerating or if he continued to play mind games with others. But this game was unlike the pursuit of attending Harvard. In this case, there was no need for exaggeration.

Mules' smug complacency of a satisfied man with a job well done did not appear to be either overstated or devious.

Their vehicle began slowing down and had to groan to a complete stop before a truck that was blocking the road on the curve in front of them.

Perry E. Zenon

The prison bus had started on LA-66 very early in the morning, battling the heavy fog from the river to avoid traffic and obstacles such as the one now confronting it.

At this hour, there were few motorists traveling this highway. In spite of its travel artery importance, it felt and appeared to be isolated and the two vehicles were quite alone.

The driver of the prison bus called in the situation, a special code for prisoner break, as two still-unseen men from the wood line rapidly approached the bus from sides, the side and the median. Their timing to arrive at the bus was perfectly synchronized.

"By the way," Mules breathlessly stated as he rapidly got down as far as he could in his seat before anyone else did, as though he knew. "This would be a good time to get your head down before you lose it."

Within a split second, the two approaching men opened rapid, staccato fire on the thin-skinned bus. Their automatic rifles were aimed at an angle to attempt to avoid hitting certain inmates--actually one. They could be certain that only guards were in the very front. There was no more morning silence.

A once quiet, if not disquieting day was bombarded by severe sounds of shells falling to the pavement, piercing the skin of the bus, with a bark that continuously exploded from the weapons. In response, metal squealed from the repeatedly punctured bus, even as it was penetrated.

As the thick bullets shattered through the bus, one shattered glass allowed entrance to side of the driver's

Hearts

head and exit through the vehicle's top. Three more rounds followed, splaying open his torso.

The two other guards scrambled in confusion, trying to figure out how to spare their own lives. Their uniforms became saturated red as the bullets easily found their bodies, deeply piercing and leaving holes splashing and oozing blood in their wake. Their bodies collapsed in the flow, shaking as they went into terminal medical shock.

While the huge bullets, the size of small missiles, projected their way toward the back of the bus in an arc pattern, the other prisoners, still tragically bound together, awkwardly tried to make themselves one with the floor.

As a bullet sped in through his window, grazed his collar bone and penetrated his throat, blood spurted out of the neck of the rapist who was sitting behind the guards. Once the sound of the last shell hitting the ground deteriorated, the pathetic, gasping gurgle of a former macho rapist, trying to breathe in the mixture of air and blood, filled the acrid void.

There was a reactive smell in the closed area, like combinations of gun powder and death in a war. The movie-like scene had revolted into death. The foggy, cotton candy aura was saturated with bright red, turning darker as it oxidized and splattered, turning the movie into the genre of horror.

The violent duo entered the ripped bus, easily snagged the keys off the lifeless, open-eyed guards, opened the separation gate, and headed to where Mules and Mitch were seated.

Perry E. Zenon

"No more time to waste," Mules said as his shackles were being unlocked.

"What 'bout him?" The muscle of the duo pointed toward Mitch, asking while he unlocked the cuffs around Mules' ankles.

"Man, I sure be happy if you'd just undo these cuffs," Mitch cut in, trying to score his own freedom before it was too late.

While the muscled invader tended to Mules, his counterpart walked to the back, intending to give the other set of keys to a soul mate inmate and let him unlock himself. Then, if he thought about it, he could helpfully pass the key to someone else.

"He's coming too," Mules had decided.

Rapidly, Mitch and Mules were completely unhitched and they leapt off the bus as two separate persons once again.

Responding to the bus driver guard's call, distant sirens' screams could be faintly heard approaching the site. The four men headed to the waiting vehicle on the other side of the semi-truck that was blocking the road. They began to put grim distance between themselves and the truck as they raced toward freedom. Once a safe distance was met, and the men entered the waiting vehicle, Muscles looked in the mirror to expertly determine if the hastily rigged explosives were enough to deter any potential prison personnel from following.

Without further hesitation, he triggered the explosives.

The inmates tumbled in unison off the bus, fell to the ground, and piled in a heap on the ground as the truck

Hearts

burst into flames, sending shrapnel into the air. The truck's cab top flew off and crashed to the ground with a lingering bang as it landed only inches from one of the inmates' head. He had initially furtively tried following Mules and his comrades in hopes they would lead him to a path of freedom, forgetting he was tied to everybody until unlocked.

Quickly, the follower was back on his feet. After making the sign of the cross in gratitude, he weighed his options and decided to follow the other inmates, now fully unshackled with the magic key. They were already into the surrounding woods and were branching off in different directions in erratic, individual escape routes.

The sounds of the sirens each wound down into silence as the squad cars arrived at the bus and saw the last of the inmates frantically trying to make it into the tree line.

"You two don't go any farther. Sheriff," a voice stated over the cruiser's intercom.

Upon hearing the command, the two inmates hesitated, but in a renewed burst of tasting freedom, decided to take a chance, and they continued. One of the patrollers radioed in a 2-10 that all of the prisoners had escaped and backup was needed. The officers on the scene headed into the woods after the prisoners, weapons drawn.

They were looking blindly because they couldn't know that after hours of searching, two of the escaped prisoners could not be found. Once their names were discovered, someone or some bodies and their heads would be out of a job.

Perry E. Zenon

"Arise, shine;
for thy light is come,
and the glory of the Lord
is risen upon thee."

Isaiah 60:1

Hearts

Chapter 2

The alarm screeched an old, annoying timbre as it erupted its signal. The tired, grating noise reverberated throughout the bedroom in search of any occupants who dared to be sleep at this hour.

I reflexively jerked up in bed, staring into the gloom of this world while still in a state of sleep fog. The raucous jangling jolted me into my world that was dark, harsh and different from the comfort of what my subconscious could create. As my eyes adjusted to the degree of darkness, my surroundings became more visible, and confusion escaped me when I realized that I had awakened from a heavy dream I couldn't remember.

I looked at the clock, making sure no one set the alarm an hour early as a cruel joke. I switched the alarm to the off position and pushed the sheets away from me

Hearts

in order to stretch my legs preliminary to getting out of bed.

Briefly, I straightened the sheets before making my way to the adjoining bathroom and open door. The reflection of the light off the tile stung my tired eyes, forcing me to turn my face away to allow them more time for reentry adjustment.

I entered the bathroom and was confronted with an obviously inaccurate mirror image of a somewhat handsome man, white but tanned, in his early forties who appears to have lived a relatively stress free life. It is said that mirrors don't lie, but I found it hard to believe that this homicide detective has had a stress-free life.

I showered, shaved, and brushed my teeth before leaving the bathroom. I always used the original Crest. It gave me a comforting link to my history. Fastidiously flossing was also an imperative. I don't like missing details, and don't intend to.

Upon exiting, I noticed that, once again, my suit ritualistically had been taken out of the closet and lovingly lay on the bed for me to wear.

I stared at the garment as a mixture of anger and happiness spread through my body, ending in my chest that tightened unbearably. My wife, Heather, my chocolate love, had always put my clothes out for me when I went in to the shower. One day I had asked her why she took out my clothes as if I were a child and she simply replied that it made her feel needed. In the eighteen months since my wife passed away, my suit had never failed to find its way to the bed and bring me love.

I glanced over at my wife's side of the bed and said, "Thank you," out of habit and out of the hope that a simple verbal gesture would bring her back to me. A year and a half of loss hadn't eased the pain. Some days I'd bring up the pain first and then her face would become more clear to me.

I got dressed, put on my shoes, and headed to the kitchen to get something to eat before going to work. As I passed by my daughter's door, I stopped and peeked inside from habit and protection, checking to make sure she wasn't still in the bed.

"Daddy, your eggs are getting cold," Eve-Marie sung out as she heard the door to her bedroom open.

I walked down the hall towards the kitchen. As I was turning the corner, the familiar, sweet smell of morning snuggled into my nose and I could hear the crackling of the grease from breakfast sausage frying on the white, chipped porcelain gas stove.

"You know that I am supposed to be the one taking care of you," I scolded as she industriously skipped around the kitchen like a Carmel Elf in a workshop.

"But, Daddy," she was amused, demonstrating her unique and precious girlish-woman giggle-laugh, "Mom left me in charge. I'm the woman of the house now, and besides I'm a way better cook."

Although womanly in attitude and response, she was dressed as a young teen for whom a wardrobe isn't paramount. Her jeans were stylishly flared over her

Hearts

leather sandals and her T-shirt had lettering that said, "Need Help? Ask A Woman."

"What's wrong with your uniform?" I noticed that she didn't have on her uniform from Academy of the Sacred Heart; The Rosary to most everybody.

"We have a field trip today, remember? We are allowed to wear what we want." She turned off the fire under the skillet. "As long as what we wear is in good taste," she rhetorically sang.

I had forgotten. Even though Heather, a former Baptist who followed through with her promise to the parish priest to raise our children Catholic, was gone, I found it hard to remember that I was totally responsible for keeping track of our little swirl.

"Okay, okay. Just don't forget that you are only thirteen. Don't let me turn into your life. Go out, have fun, do what kids your age are doing before it's too late."

I humorously reconsidered the advice I gave as I remembered the things kids were doing these days-- pink and green hair. They resembled big troll dolls.

"Too late for what?" She turned around with a plate in either hand and placed them on the table.

"To be a kid," I informed her as I pulled out the chair where she left my plate and sat next to me.

"Da-ad-d-y, nothing is interfering with me being a kid. I just want to help you out a little, that's all," she tactfully responded to my early morning blahs.

Eve-Marie was teasingly piqued, sweetly patronizing me as only the women in my family know how. She crossed herself and bowed her head to bless her food.

Perry E. Zenon

Her mother would have been pleased. I couldn't bring myself to honor the God who had taken Heather.

I ate my breakfast without the slightest notion that the eggs were too runny, the grits were too thick, or that the sausage was almost burnt.

"Better overdone than not done," I reassured my gut. As much as I tried to remain true to Heather's values and eat right, I was still pretty used to greasy fast foods. A job expediency, I'd say whenever she inquired about what I ate during lunch.

I glanced up to see Eve-Marie trying to eat while studying for a final test. I knew I was to blame for her taking on too much responsibility, and I hoped, as I often did when feeling twinges of guilt, that just because we named her Life-Bitter she won't end up living the bitter part of life.

For a moment, I could see Heather sitting with us, beaming her gorgeous, open smile and looking approvingly at the family scene. It was nice that no pain accompanied this moment.

She said to my mind, "You see, we did such a good job. We can be so proud of our baby, a year ahead in school, taking advanced classes and already deciding to be a nurse to help humanity, too." Heather had been a social worker.

I took the dishes and loaded them into the dishwasher, setting the cycle to run while we were gone. I took the keys off the hook as we were going out the door.

Hearts

*****

Traffic is still slow this time of the morning and South Broad Avenue's only motorist was in a black sedan turning into a parking lot. Across the street from where the car turned, three seemingly colorless pedestrians waited at the bus stop.

The bus stop may have appeared mundane, but the people were interacting. A high school student sat on the bench with his backpack beside him, having to ride thebus for the first time this year after wrapping his car around a telephone pole.

"What time does this bus get here, did I miss it?" the student wondered aloud.

"It should have gotten here by now. I don't know what's taking this driver so long," Loretta crankily complained while pacing in front of the bench. She was a youngish, middle-aged black woman accustomed to taking responsibility for working hard and being on time.

She recently landed the position as senior housekeeper for the hotel, and after pulling a double watching after the younger girls on the shift, her patience was minimal.

Jamie Beales blended into the signpost with her long, largely unkempt medium to dark, mousy blonde hair andnondescript clothing. She inhaled her cigarette smoke, casually watching the woman as she paced, while patiently leaning against the bus stop sign. Beales had a mission to accomplish, but it was nothing that couldn't wait five or ten minutes for the bus to arrive.

Perry E. Zenon

"It's about time," Janice harrumphed, stopping her pacing when she saw the bus turning the corner toward them.

Unlike the avenue's car lanes at this time of morning, the bus was crowded with people who had no other means of transportation, or perhaps were practical. The doors opened and a male in his thirties looked out from the driver's seat.

"What took you so long? Don't you know people want to go home after work?" Loretta questioned impatiently.

"Are you gettin' on or what?" the driver grumbled. "It's people like you what make me late." His muscles inadvertently flexed under his gray uniform as he moved.

"If you would drive the bus more and sleep less you wouldn't be late," she retorted, climbing the bus steps.

"And if you would walk more and ride my bus less you wouldn't have to worry bout it."

"Good morning," Jamie greeted the driver before taking the only empty seat left on the bus next to a man who turned his head towards the window to limit how much he had to smell the residual stench of her smoking.

*****

I dropped Eve-Marie off at The Rosary High School before I went to work at the New Orleans Police Department on South Broad Avenue where the only thing that seemed to change was the perpetrator and the victim.

Nowadays you can't even count on women being the ones who are battered, or that substance abuse is to blame.

It will be fifteen years next month that I have been working here and advanced to a detective in the homicide division nine years ago.

I got out of the car and began to take control of the rest of my morning preparation leading to the fully alert stage.

A slight breeze came in from the Mississippi River, supplying temporary relief until the sun starts to beat down on the day. I enjoyed the cool morning and threw my keys up in the air and caught them repeatedly as I walked to the door. I knew the temperature would soar throughout this late May day and the sixty-seven per-cent humidity would make it feel a lot hotter than it actually was. Next month there would be heat warnings.

I came closer to the door and noticed three officers in a circle outside the entrance to the building. They seemed to be awestruck while viewing a smallish brown box from a bit of a distance.

Every person in the system must attend and pass the rigorous Police Officers' Training Academy. Part of the program teaches personnel to carefully examine packages and letters in their homes and on the system's property. This package was not glued in places, had no leaking oil, no careful, square lettering--in fact, it had no lettering at all except one name.

Perry E. Zenon

"It's not a bomb." An officer announced the almost obvious as he bent down to pick up the box.

The other two stepped back and covered their face as if they still expected shards of cardboard and metal to explode in their direction.

"It's just a package," he affirmed.

"Well, it's too early for normal deliveries, and this one didn't come in no mail; I ain't no fool. Do you watch the news?" the young officer muttered rhetorically while taking a step backward.

"Man, people dying from pipe bombs and letter bombs and car bombs, it could be a trick."

Their POST training had included unforgettable videos of the 1985 devastation of the Hoffman bombings in Utah.

"Hey, they have better ways to do that now!" The officer holding the box stopped and read the label.

"You know a Detective Jack Callow?" he inquired as he walked back toward the other two. "This package is addressed to him."

"I think he's in..."

"That's me," I interrupted abruptly, coming along beside them. "My name is Jack Callow."

The patrolman handed me the box and went inside after his two comrades. I didn't follow behind them but instead stood outside staring at the box, processing its familiar size and lettering as a wave of nausea flushed through me. The same feeling always came over me now when I received a package at the office. There was only one person I can think of who has sent me a package at this location.

Hearts

Larry Mules.

Larry Mules was my last major and ongoing assignment, lasting over three years, but he should be starting to rot in prison. After over three years of intensive work, with the help of my partner I was finally able to close this file. The jury found him guilty and he was sentenced to life without parole. I know the process can take a couple of days sometimes, but he should have been transferred to Angola in Feliciana Parish by now.

I still remember reading the headlines stating The Heart Taker Plucks Another. The media really had a way to make things sound mundane.

That sick psychopath would always remove the heart of his latest victim and then send me his token prize. As if he imagined I had an appreciation for his line of work and kept a collection.

The day seemed to get wildly colder as I turned the package around in my hand, furtively searching for a return address, a note, or anything else that would ease my troubled mind that desperately wished that a heart was not the contents.

That serenity wasn't available.

There's always some copycat dope trying to mimic a serial killer, I hoped.

I rationalized, "I'm sure one just couldn't wait to dupe this one, probably trying to lead the cops on to thinking that they convicted the wrong person or that there could now be two serial killers like in the horror movies."

I was, frankly, feeling confused.

Perry E. Zenon

I couldn't find any identifying markings anywhere, just a neat, clean, computer-generated white label boldly bearing my name.

I opened the door to take a step inside my safe domain and then stopped.

Things just felt odd, baffling, like the beginning of a threatening day.

The door seemed to stall by itself as it struck me that, in the past, the packages from Larry Mules always came in normal post office mail delivery.

This realization didn't ease my troubled mind at all.

Hearts

Perry E. Zenon

Chapter 3

The sun began slowly beating down on the grass,
intensifying while it cooked the blades as it does when
water evaporates, instead of being able to be consumed
by thirsting plants. The slight tit, tit, tit of the sprinklers
running in the yards throughout the neighborhood
could
be heard as they dispensed water in a semicircular
motion.

The residents set their sprinklers before leaving for
work, failing to realize that watering the lawn while the
sun was out only wasted water and damaged the grass
rather than helping.

A white van stopped at the corner of the street. It was
part of a rental company's fleet that had been purchased

Hearts

at an auction when the company retired their older vehicles.

The decals featuring the rental company were easily scraped away, allowing the van to be used for any kind of personal use. The van turned the corner and pulled along the sidewalk in front of the only brick house on the street.

The driver turned off the ignition and reached over to grab a gray clipboard from the passenger's side before getting out of the van. The sturdy, metal clipboard contained a compartment underneath. It used to store job documents or anything else needed to be handy for jobs.

The driver got out, traveled the walkway leading to the house, climbed the steps up to the porch, and rang the doorbell. No one responded within the allotted fifteen seconds and impatiently the button was repeatedly pushed, ringing the tinny, musical doorbell that played a sad, abbreviated rendition of the Westminster chimes.

"Who is it?" A soft voice came from the other side of the door.

"I'm here from the cable company, ma'am. I'm here to install your cable," the representative crisply replied in a friendly, low voice.

"Hold on a second," louder this time.

The cable representative heard a jarring orchestra of three locks being disengaged.

"May I see some identification please?" Dena Guidry briskly inquired as she peered through the glass of the storm door.

Perry E. Zenon

The representative unclipped the ID card dangling from the shirt pocket, correctly placing it up to the security bars for the lady's inspection. After discovering no obvious sign of forgery, and ensuring the picture matched the slender-faced cable guy, Dena opened the storm door as the representative pulled the ID back through the bars.

"Whoa, wait here," Dena said, realizing she did not have the key to the security gate.

"Sorry to have to make you go through all of this, but you kin never be to careful now days. 'Sides, ya just don't strike me as a cable guy or whatever it is y'all call yourselves these days. My husband is always telling me about the horrors he has read in the newspaper." Dena airily fluffed when she came back with the key to the gate.

"Come on in."

To the right, just inside the entrance, was the living room featuring a brown faux leather living room set, endand coffee tables in dark oak, a modern, silver standing lamp, and a new light oak entertainment center with a complete Panasonic home theater system.

"We want cable in this room." Dena indicated the living room with her hand then pointed towards the rear of the house. "And the room in back, although I don't know why, cause when we are back there we're not watching television." Dena smiled coyly.

The representative was unresponsive.

To the rear of the living room was a remodeled archway that led to what appeared to be a small dining room connected to the kitchen that had a door leading to the yard. To the left of the living room, the cable rep could see a hall that accessed the remainder of the house.

"Can you show me which one of the rooms in the back? I need to run the wires outside first."

"Yeah, sure, this way."

As Dena led the way to the back of the house, the cable guy quickly opened the compartment in the metal clipboard, extracted a handkerchief, and opened a small bottle of chloroform. After saturating the handkerchief with the chloroform, the cable rep quickly walked behind Dena.

"This is a lovely house you have here."

"Thank you, we..."

As Dena started to turn her head back to be heard, the cable guy grabbed her arm, awkwardly jerked her to the floor, and placed the chloroform-soaked cloth over her face. The assailant took pains to avoid the fumes while struggling with the victim.

Quickly realizing what had happened, Dena vigorously struggled, trying to free herself from her assailant. She was street savvy and deliberately tried to scratch the cable guy for potential police evidence. But with each breath she drew for energy, she inhaled the substance more and her resistance dwindled.

Dena's limbs sporadically flailed as she sunk and slowly, helplessly fell unconscious. And the cable guy let her body sprawl on the floor.

Standing now, the cable rep glared down at Dena while straightening the uniform and repositioning the company cap over the almost blond hair.

Perry E. Zenon

*****

As I drew closer to the office door, I could hear the voices of others going on about something and getting louder.

There, standing in the hall, was an average man. He wasn't someone all the ladies initially would dream for, neither were they appalled by him. It didn't matter. His hair was black like soot, streaked with a bit of ash and looked, as did many officers, as if he always used a military barber. Detective Smith, who had joined the military to pay his way through college, was still rugged looking. A hefty, almost trim, tall black man, square in frame, he looked as if he'd boxed for the early part of the forty-four years he had been alive, and he had.

Dean Smith and I have been partners for nine years. I have to trust someone with my life on a regular basis. I'm just glad it's him.

"Hey bro, did you listen to the news?" One   thing about Dean Smith, he was up on his current affairs. He was always gossiping about what had just happened. If we had just declared war on Mother England, or a lady went berserk and murdered her family before doing herself, he would be one of the first to know. And he wouldn't hesitate to share.

"Yeah, we lost a plane over in China or something," I said distractedly, trying to end the morning news report.

"No, a couple prisoners `scaped over the weekend. And the bus was bombed."

This came across bad to me. I mean it's not out of the ordinary to have a couple escapees, but to have Dean

Hearts

Smith call it news? Now that is unusual. `Course, no bombings are taken lightly today.

"So, I'm not going look for them, Dean."

With the same feeling in my gut as when I picked up the package, I was hoping he just didn't have anything better to greet me with.

"I think you will want to when you find out one of their names."

I felt an incredible, total body reentry of the big chill as he spoke the last of those words.

Was this a coincidence?

I studied the package that I now held tightly in my hand, as if the pressure from my fingertips could change the contents in the same manner that ugly coal is transformed into a diamond.

"Dean, this package was outside with my name on it." I sadly looked up from the package and into his dark, perceptive eyes.

"God, tell me this isn't happening again."

I took the delay of an answer to only mean the worst and went around him to take the package in the office. I now urgently needed to open it and get through my worst, repeating nightmare.

Prior to my arrival, Dean must have told everyone in the office because the moment I walked through the door conversations stopped. All eyes were upon me, sympathetically trying to read my response to the escape.

The younger officers moved silently to the side. Some were still behind me, perhaps curious to view the suspected contents of the box.

Hearts

I placed the box on the handiest desk, treating it like the proverbial hot potato.

It sickened me to think of the efforts we all had to go through and the nights I carried the puzzle of his crimes home in my head. And then he escapes? Maybe not, I fleetingly hoped.

I stared at the wicked box with dread, but I knew the unveiling had to be. As with each of the other packages after the first one, I didn't adhere to the extra precautionary warnings of using the bomb squad, and I opened the box.

No one came to close to my desk. Maybe the contents could still explode in my face; maybe the impending reality was too horrifying, even for some of the seasoned officers and staff.

Then Dean walked up beside me, absolutely fearless of the nonexistent bomb. He leaned over the desk to observe for himself what was inside.

I snatched the box off the desk and tore foolishly at the side, ripping it open. The perpetrator was not going to win. Any fear I felt had turned to anger. I admitted to myself what the box's contents would be.

The container was open.

Although one quick glance was enough to see what it was, I stood staring in disbelief at the ziplock bag that I knew held the heart of Larry Mules' most recent victim. He had murdered once more and regaled me with his trophy.

I slumped with pain at the desk and placed my head in my hands, very sick to my stomach while my fellow officers, most of whom had never encountered a true psychopath's works, slowly attempted to take back their day through small-talk bravado.

"OK, so he's at it again." Dean, a solidly built black man with strong fingers and hands, placed a firm hand on my shoulder for tangible support. "We caught him once. We just have to do it again."

"Yes. I know. I hate that it's starting over. Another dead woman. Like my Heather. Another reason for the community to live in terror again," I sadly reminded him.

I moved to open this case again and started to take the package down the dingy stairs to the lab technician for organ tissue matching.

Reaching the doorway, an imposing, tall, robust man who has been at this game a little too long entered. While his figure was obviously shifting and he had less hair than when younger, Chief Pitre still maintained an attractive quality.

"Where you going?" Chief asked, assuming I was leaving the building.

"I'm just taking the new addition from Mules' trophies downstairs to see if we can get a match."

"The news was late in getting to us. I'm going to have somebody's head. I just heard that he escaped early yesterday." My chief was furious.

"You know his game, the psycho has to make sure I know that he's out," I grimly replied.

Already my day took me in a direction I didn't intend or, what's worse for a detective, didn't even remotely expect, nor was able to control. I headed out the door and down the hall to the stairs. My very being was

Hearts

decaying from fear for the unknown woman; and there was the accompanying rage. My package wasn't the only thing that was rotting.

*****

The bass from a stereo system vibrated the walls of the apartment complex. With her arms full of grocery bags, Loretta Walker carefully climbed the stairs leading to her apartment on the second floor. Before leaving for work, she had asked her oldest son to go get some things from the store, but as usual he neglected to do so and, in turn, asked her to stop on her way home.

Seeing his mother approaching the building, LJ courteously opened the door because her hands were full.

"I know you not gonna just stand there. Boy, if you don't come get these bags..."

"Look like you had `em."

"You should have `em; I carried `em from the bus stop. The least you can do is put them in the house."

"OK, OK." LJ took the bags from Janice and sat them on the kitchen floor.

"Boy, if you don't put them groceries away, I swear." Loretta was tired and exasperated.

She walked over to the closet and grabbed a broom; holding it towards the bottom, she hit the tip of it against the ceiling.

"Turn that mess off."

Hearing no difference in the volume, she hit harder.

"Don't make me come up there." She gave up on the broom and returned it to the closet. "Every morning it's the same thing. LJ, go up there and tell that girl to turn that crap off."

"But you told me..."

"Now I'm tellin' you to go up there, you can put that away when you get back." She began walking to the bedroom.

LJ went up the stairs to the above apartment as his mother instructed. The stairs shook under his weight as he took them two at a time. After he reached the landing, LJ went directly to the door and banged on it over the percussion coming from within.

"Ms. Mary, Mom said to turn the music off. Ms. Mary."

With no response, LJ resorted to kicking the door in order to be heard over the music.

"Ms. Mary, open up."

The door opened and LJ looked down to see Ms. Mary's youngest child standing there.

"Ms. Mary, if you don't turn it off, she's gonna call the cops again," LJ shouted over the youth.

"My mommy can't talk to you."

"What, she in the shower or somethin'?"

"No, she dead."

"Boy, quit playin'," LJ insisted as he looked down at the somber child, suddenly seeing he was covered in blood.

"Ma!" LJ screamed for assistance.

Chapter 4

After Dena was ruthlessly bound and gagged, gasping and flailing, her attacker, still posing as the cable guy, moved the utility van to the side of the house and gathered up equipment for installation.

This cover was for the neighbors' police reports. If they saw that someone from the cable company had come to the house, there would be suspicion if cable had not been installed. The perpetrator was trying to stifle further inquiry. It was a small ruse, but the cable guy felt it to be a significant piece of cleverness.

The previous tenants already had cable installed in the house. The connections were still present, making the job fairly easy when only having to activate the lines and connect the receivers to the televisions.

Perry E. Zenon

After connecting the cable in the master bedroom and the living room, the cable guy nonchalantly grasped and dragged Dena's helpless body through the dining room to the back door. The intruder viewed with satisfaction the physical notice that she'd not retained her control.

Although the lock was released, the door still wouldn't slide open when the attacker pulled on the handle. The aggressor had to use both hands in order to slide open the door that squealed and jerked from friction and accumulated dirt between the metal door and the groove it slid on. The door led to an enclosed patio, which occupied the majority of the overgrown, fenced-in yard.

While taking the tools to the van, the representative carefully surveyed the area to ensure there were no prying eyes at a window. Then the guy returned to the house for Dena. Although the victim was not a heavy woman, the attacker's shirt became damp with both perspiration and sprinkler mist while hauling Dena out of the patio area, struggling to unceremoniously stuff her into the back of the van.

Dena moved reactively. Immediately, the rag was alertly saturated and placed over her mouth and nose, rending her unconscious and vulnerable once more. The cable guy, appearing casual, checked the area again for witnesses before walking around to the driver's door and climbing in behind the wheel of the van.

The van cautiously pulled away from Dena's home, and the sprinkler's tic, tic, tic faded.

Hearts

*****

The stairs to our venerable, sometimes putrid-smelling, precinct crime laboratory wound down to an old, heavy wooden door that led to the lab. I immediately spotted a man in a traditional white lab coat sitting behind a table. When Rogers saw me, he began

waving both hands in the air trying to make me go back.

Ignoring his ridiculous plea for me to stop, I kept walking, pushed the doors fully open. Without regard for its contents, I plopped the box onto the countertop.

"Don't you ever listen?" Roger, the fixture, said as he passed his hand through his unkempt blonde, gray-streaked hair.

"Never did, why should I start today?"

I was glumly responding to my friend with whom I'd had very close contact during this case for three years. I slowly slid the box across to him.

"I heard the news," Rogers picked up the box. "Just didn't think the perp would start this again so soon after breaking out."

He walked from behind the counter and stood next to me. As an above-average-size man, roughly between six and six-two, I couldn't help but compare myself to Rogers' ladder-like seven feet two inches. I felt as if I were one of the diminutives in a Lollipop Gang.

"Is there anything you already know on this one?" Rogers asked, pulling out the sturdy ziplock bag.

"Nope, found it outside the office. See what you can figure out and let me know, pronto."

Perry E. Zenon

"Man, this guy is the only person that can make me squeamish."

"You?" I exaggerated in looking at Rogers from head to toe. "You probably could step on him without much of an effort, my gentle, intellectual, bruiser of a friend."

*****

As the van pulled into the driveway, the garage door opener received the signal generated by the remote. The motor issued a soft hum as the door slowly began to ascend. The van pulled into the garage. The motor reversed, lowering the door when the signal was delivered.

Speckles of light illuminated the interior of the garage through the paint- and dirt-caked windows in the garage door. The driver's side door opened. The abductor exited the vehicle, walked to the wall by the stairs, and turned on the lights. A fluorescent light flickered above a stainless steel table, illuminating the tomblike confines of the garage.

The driver opened the rear doors on the van, revealing a once attractive and assertive Dena Guidry lying helplessly unconscious in the cargo hold, both bound and gagged. The driver tightly grabbed Dena under her arms, with effort dragging her, bumping out of the van elevation, then over to the table. She was helplessly restrained at the waist, ankles, and wrists with old leather straps encrusted with cleaned dried blood andgrime that were affixed to the table, waiting for her.

Hearts

Dena began to regain consciousness and had a zingy taste in her mouth from the chloroform used to knock her unconscious. The perpetrator crammed a wad of rags into Dena's mouth in anticipation and saw that she was drowsily awakening. Her eyes opened a bit, but vision was blurred and straining; she saw only a fog.

"You gave your heart to your husband, to Robert," the driver began, knowing Dena couldn't see the person who leaned menacingly in front of her eyes. Dena reactively recoiled from a breath that had turned fetid from the mouth's dryness created by an adrenaline high.

Harshly, "Does Robert know where you are when he goes out of town?"

Although significantly drowsy, the question was so intimate, so bizarre, that the response was a physical jump.

Although it was impossible to see the person, she could smell the rancid body and hear the increasing acceleration of the pitch of the voice and the rapidity of the frantic words. Her instincts were still intact, but her body refused to follow.

Still confused, Dena looked around the room, trying to recognize or gain help from her blurred surroundings. On a stand next to the table, the light made the stainless steel of the tools glistened. The driver methodically put on latex hospital gloves, picked up a contaminatedscalpel, and held it up to the light, looking it over before placing it back down and picking up a bigger one.

"You tell Robert that you are at your mother's while he is gone."

Perry E. Zenon

The abductor was oozing crisp, blunt sarcasm, the kind that packs a spine full of chills.

After a tight-lipped smile over the scalpel, the abductor turned to precisely select another with more killing power.

Demanding, sarcastic, "Was that your mother's house you were at earlier, Dena?"

Now even more alarmed because her name was known and she was an obvious target of probably a stalker and certainly an abductor, she squinted in the direction of the voice, now further away, trying to ascertain where it was coming from. Dena was concentrating while fighting to focus enough to see who it was, if there could be an escape route, and what the kidnapper seemed occupied with.

As her vision slowly cleared, she recognized the slim, open face of the cable guy. In keeping with the innocent look, blond or light brown hair tailings peeked out from under some of the company cap.

Confused, she didn't understand what her attacker's reasons for the rhetorical but frighteningly accurate questions were, but she was unwilling to answer for fear it would be the wrong one.

"I don't think the name that was on the cable requisition form was a lady's name," the throaty voice gloated, lovingly toying the tools on the cloth, ignoring her.

The body suddenly turned from the table with a satisfied selection in hand.

The perpetrator smoothly, breathlessly said, "Once you give someone your heart it is no longer yours."

Hearts

Straining, she could catch the view of an object in a hand. Horrified, Dena was consumed with fear and began to uncontrollably tremble.

The physiological flight or fight response suddenly exacerbated. She didn't want to show that she felt vulnerable and terrorized because she felt calmness was her only hope with this maniac. But, it overcame her; there was no more attempted pretense. She shook in every cell of her body including her teeth as she frantically, openly pulled against the restraints, trying desperately to free herself.

"You gave your heart to Robert and I shall see to it that he gets it," the driver taunted.

Dena briefly clamped her eyes tightly shut to escape the ugly, horrifying dream she fully knew she was in.

She experienced the last shred of her assertiveness when she emitted her last, agonizingly piercing, gagged scream as the psychopath made a shallow, stabbing incision and began chiseling open her chest.

*****

Larry Mules had been a pitch fork in my side for three years and I was ready to be relieved of the pain-- again. Mules didn't make many mistakes and I'm sure that if he hadn't been seen with the body of his last victim we would still have few clues about who was responsible for the murders.

Except we remind ourselves that we always catch even the smart ones because their egos won't allow them to fade away. They need to be noticed; hence, the trophy reminders the savage sent to me.

"These rats are driving me up a wall," a female lamented. Her softly educated but strong voice could be heard coming from and trailing down the hallway.

Detective Jade Knowles entered the office in an easy, athletic glide and placed her clipboard on her desk by the door. She glanced over at me with those sometimes cool, startling clear green eyes and then, as if she considered him a threat, she went over to the door as her partner was coming through it.

"You are not going to catch him that easy, you know. He be too smart for this," Detective Cain Xavier stated to her, entering the office.

Detective Xavier had been Knowles' partner for a year since he had been upgraded from patrol officer and passed his exam on the force. He has yet to have an optimistic outlook on anything.

After a year of working together, Detectives Knowles and Xavier had developed a respectful working relationship which few would understand. They reminded me of siblings. They might fight often amongst themselves, but when times require it, they seriously back each other.

"Don't even start with me, Cain," Jade demanded, turning away from him and going to the water cooler.

"I'm just saying he's smart, that's all," Detective Xavier said. Although he is a local boy, his ancestry dates to Germany. With light skin, his black hair de-notes the characterization of Black German. He's almost six foot tall and built like a solid, tidy mule.

Hearts

Detective Knowles is the only female in the homicide division and currently she is the only female detective to have lasted longer than six months. I'm not too sure what it is, but not long after they arrive, the females receive a transfer to Jefferson Parrish Police Department.

"So how's my little friend been doing?" Jade referred to my Eve-Marie while standing in front of my desk with her arms folded, feet slightly apart, testing balance, demonstrating athletic readiness and strength.

Due to the increased murders in the New Orleans area, the precinct was required to expand its homicide division, moving seasoned officers into detective slots, and Detective Knowles had joined as a rookie during the expansion. She progressed rapidly. Her major had been criminology.

When she later arrived at my precinct after a time of being an officer then passing a very difficult test, none of the macho detectives wanted to work with her while she became familiar with the area and the position she would fill.

They didn't seem to be able to get their brains and emotions around both her green-eyed, lithe, creamy African-American/Asian/Anglo beauty's smarts and the fact that she was an advanced Tae Kwon Doe black belt.

When Dean Smith was forced to take a few sick days, Jade filled in as my partner on a case I was working. On the second day, I had to pick-up Eve-Marie from school when her mother wasn't able to and Jade rode with me. Jade talked to my little girl on a level I wasn't able to reach, and they began chatting as if they were old girlfriends. Ever since that day, Jade has referred to Eve-Marie as her little friend.

"She has been great." I rose from my desk.

"She tries too hard to take care of the house, and she is doing a woman's job and I worry about her having play time, too."

As I was trying to talk to Jade, and her partner was occupied with files, Dean was standing behind her waving his silly hand in the air to catch my attention.

"I heard Mules was out and already sent you a package. Are you sure that it was him?"

I couldn't help but look at Dean's antics while Jade was talking.

"She wants you." He exaggeratedly mouthed this inanity so I could understand what he was trying to tell me. As if his frantic pointing between us wasn't enough. If he were seen, his teasing would be uncomfortable. Come to think of it, it was anyway.

Jade is a friend. Eve-Marie wasn't handling the loss of her mother too well and she wasn't opening up to me about how she was feeling. It was hard for me to know where to begin with a child--not a girl, but certainly not a woman either. I asked Jade to see if she could get through to her and she came through for me. Ever since then, the precinct's gossip column always found a way to insinuate that Jade and I had a thing for each other.

I wasn't sure why God had lowered his sights on me, taking away one of the two people I had loved more than anything earthly, but I was not going to give Him another way to harm me. Loving again was out of the question. I just couldn't handle another close person's death. Not an option. God just hadn't been there for me. Big broken promises.

"I don't know how he moved so quickly, but he has, and I need you and Dean to find him fast," Chief demanded as he walked in on the tail of our conversation.

"They found him once. It's keeping him that appears to be the detectives' recent problem," Xavier knowingly butted in.

"What are you two working on?" Chief barked while glaring from Knowles to Xavier.

"They're trying to catch a rat that's too smart for them, but we will have Mules again as soon as we can find a place to start looking," interjected Detective Dean Smith, my partner, with a twist of humor.

"Well, how about starting by looking at the body that was just found?" Chief asked.

"Our female victim had a perfectly removed heart taken from her body before her death."

The news was accepted with a tremendous sinking feeling. Another woman we didn't protect and serve.

Chief was obviously feeling the grimness of the situation too. He was personally affronted that our perp was terrifying citizens once again.

"And you two leave the rat-catching to the exterminators. I have something I need you to look into."

Chief handed a printout to Xavier, who reached over and snatched the paper out of his hands, leaving him with just the corner between his thumb and forefinger.

"Oh, and by the way."

Perry E. Zenon

Off guard, we all looked toward our Chief, and respectfully waited for him to finish his statement as he stood near his office door.

"Keep your personal lives and your professional ones separated."

He was so wrong.

Chapter 5

With noon steadily approaching, the streets came alive as motorists and walkers communed to and from restaurants, banks, and their homes in an attempt to satisfy their hunger, bills, and libidos. We didn't even have to think as we followed the road, past the Superdome to the crime scene.

"You ready for this?" I asked my partner as I turned the ignition to the off position.

"Hey bro', the fun has just begun." Dean, the jokester, darkly responded to me with his door already open.

The sun-baked grass crunched under our feet as we walked, bringing forth the realization that we were leaving prints of our feet at a murder scene. I studied the ground in a cursory manner for markings to identify footprints that were left at the site by the killer.

Perry E. Zenon

The priorities of a criminal investigation are to handle all emergencies first, secure the scene, and finally to conduct the investigation. Securing the crime scene is a major responsibility of the first officers to arrive.

I found footprints going in different directions and even some overlapping others, but nothing could be seen
identifying previous, obvious crime scene tracks. I knew this was the product of a blue-suited officer's unsophisticated inability to correctly secure the crime scene.

A young woman officer was walking toward Dean and me; or perhaps she was either trying to be like her father, scruffily dressed in his work uniform while merrily playing cops and robbers, or it was the clown rookie who was more than likely the blame for mishandling potential evidence.

"Man, have you ever seen anything like this?" the wispy, darkly streaked blonde excitedly asked once she was next to us.

"Yes, I have. I've seen over twenty others, to be almost exact."

I wasn't half as impressed with this grotesque scene as she seemed to be. After fifteen years in my work, and three years of Larry Mules' victims, I was well past the adrenaline rush of being at a murder scene.

"I'm Officer Beales. When I was doin' rounds, a suspicious neighbor stopped me and led me here."

Hearts

"I hear the guy who did this just got out of jail," this rookie, whose hair was mostly covered by her cap, stated in a low voice. Yes, she was already starting to get to me.

"Just got out? He wasn't even in yet," Dean grumbled as he walked toward her.

My wide-eyed, athletic partner seemed to sardonically enjoy entertaining the dumb questions and comments of the naïve uniformed officers, and I gladly let him interview the first officer at the scene to ascertain their theory and get information on interviews that I'd actually have to repeat anyway.

I don't know if he got his kicks watching them, or if he encouraged them to stay around just to get under my skin.

"You mean to tell me he didn't even get a chance to be inside?" Officer Beales asked in disbelief.

I wondered if this officer, actually a girl, I thought, really thought it was a waste for Mules to have escaped before experiencing the community's tax dollars' accruements. Prisoners cost way more per person than helping kids from low-income families.

In most cases, I would have waited for Dean to update me on what he had learned about any murder theory, but considering this was an area chosen only to set up, to display the victim, there probably wasn't much the officer could say that I hadn't already been exposed to.

We hadn't discovered the location where Mules removed hearts, but we knew it wasn't the area where the bodies were displayed. When I examined the scene I

Perry E. Zenon

would, frustratingly, only find blood on the body and no other apparent clues--especially good footprints in the stomped grass today. The clown was there first.

Larry Mules was a stickler for the way his murder scenes were set up and this scene was another cookie cutter of his horrific ego. The bodies were all found leaning against a tree, with their arms folded as if they were napping and unaware of the gaping hole in their chest. The latest, late female victim from today was sliced in the identical manner.

After the first victim, we realized the perpetrator was a clear-thinking psychopath, one with no remorse and no values to contain him. The time he took to make sure the minor details were the same had always indicated a supreme ego, a thrill of the challenge and a violent hatred of women. And each crime took extensive deliberations and probably stalking--a lot of effort each time.

While some might see his profile as crazy, our forensic social worker and the FBI psychologist saw him as a frighteningly rational perpetrator with absolutely no values of constraint to moderate his behaviors, who was able to carefully plan and execute his fantasies. No sympathy. No empathy and absolutely no remorse or ethical judgment that most people use to make decisions.

Searching a dead body should be done only after the coroner or medical examiner has arrived or given permission. Searching a dead body can be unpleasant even if the person died only minutes ago. I didn't see the examiner around yet.

Hearts

I wiped the sweat off my brow in a careless, unthinking motion and then photographed the scene as a record of items of possible evidence. I motioned for the guys to collect the body and walked over to Dean and rookie Beales, the mousey blonde.

"Well, I think we know who the heart from this morning belongs to."

"Heart from this morning...I don't get it," Beales admitted, looking baffled.

"Excuse me, Officer..." I began while trying to look at her badge.

"Beales." She was almost coquettish but also somewhat insincere or affected, or perhaps just stuck in adolescence.

"Right, Beales. We will go to follow-up with this case in the lab, so if you will excuse us, our job is done here and we will be leaving." I informed her and I walked away.

"Are you hungry?" Dean asked as we crunched the grass on our way to the car.

I'm not quite sure if viewing a violent crime scene is what gives him an appetite, or if we just always seem to view one around his feeding time.

"You know me, can't turn down an opportunity to put on a few pounds." I used any excuse to eat fast food.

The streets were mainly deserted now after lunch rush so it didn't take us long to get to the Mom and Pops in Sick Villa, LA. Sick Villa wasn't its actual name, just the name we gave the area immediately around the four hospitals that were located within minutes of walking distance to each other. The area swarmed with those who were sick, mostly poor people of color, and those who provided aid to the desperate and had no regular physician's services.

A little bell attached to the door tinkled as we entered the restaurant. Upon recognizing us, the skinny, old-time waitress walked to the table where we usually sat with our backs to the wall.

"Will y'all be having the usual today or ya' want the special?"

Although Gloria was in her fifties, she didn't look a day over thirty-five. She had hair of richly tinted chestnut, light brown eyes, light tanned complexion, and a face essentially free of wrinkles or blemishes. She credited her youthful appearance to years of healthy dieting, exercise from waiting tables, and skin treatment, a combination foreign to the locals in this part of the world.

"Make mine the usual," said Dean.

"And I'll have the special."

"Sure thing, hon, that's tea for him, coke for yew, right?" Gloria took up the menus.

We nodded our heads and Gloria took two sets of silverware wrapped in cloth napkins out of the pocket on
her apron and placed them along with straws on the table, then walked to the back.

The only other customer in the restaurant was a gentleman barely in his twenties, sitting in the farthest corner. The young African-American man, who was wearing a medical bracelet used to match the parents with the correct baby, was probably just out of the delivery room, using his wife's recovery period to eat and reflect on how his life had just changed now with the responsibilities he inherited. The birth of a new dependent affects everyone's family.

The new father triggered my own sweet memories thirteen years ago with Heather.

"So, he hasn't been out for forty-eight hours and we already have a stiff," Dean said to the air.

I was distracted with watching my home video in my brain, the one stored in my memory library of Eve-Marie's birth. I wasn't aware Dean was talking and that I had a social obligation to answer.

Laughing with myself, I remembered how alarmed I became when I noticed a round, purple-brown circle on the lower back of my baby girl.

The nurses quickly eased my mind when they informed me that it was common in interracial and many other ethnic babies; she called it some kind of mark. A Mongolian mark. As a white man, my experiences would have not necessarily included that piece of baby information and I was initially perplexed because my baby was not Mongolian.

"I take it I'm talking to myself," queried my sturdy black friend and colleague in his commanding, resonant, awakening voice.

"What?" I began, switching from my mind's reel back to what was currently going on.

I concentrated and replayed his statement in my head and realized I was ignoring him.

"Oh, sorry, just thinking about this case."

"It's funny how you be good at detectin' when someone else be lying, but you be so bad at it yourself,"

Perry E. Zenon

Dean laughed with himself at his exaggerated dialect as he opened his straw's sleeve.

"Here you go. I have a tuna on rye with a salad for you and ètouffèe for you," Gloria announced as she placed our plates in front of us followed by two glasses of ice which she filled with tea and soda respectively, and sat the pitchers in the center of the table.

"You boys enjoy!"

"You know, that cat food you always eat could be the reason you stay hungry." I implied, motioning towards Dean's healthy, quasi-vegetarian lunch as he prepared for eating by making the sign of the cross and I grabbed the salt.

"Tuna just a nutritious diet, but I can tell you don't know anything about eating healthy by the way you add salt to your food before you taste it. You don't even know if it is needed or not.

"If you were black, you'd be educated to know to be especially conscious of high blood pressure," Dean pointed out as he invigorated his salad with vinegar and oil dressing.

"And for your information this isn't all I eat. I'm just not fond of grease lodging in my gut."

We normally ate with a degree of silence as we concentrated on our private thoughts while we seemed to be contemplating our meals. Sometimes we broke the barrier long enough to comment on pedestrians as they pass by the window or enter the restaurant, but with the case piling up so rapidly, we couldn't get off the subject. We talked.

Hearts

"How long you think it will take for us to catch him again?" Dean asked before placing a forkful of cat food into his mouth.

Casually, seriously, "I was hoping he would just turn himself in." Usually the humor was reserved for Dean's repartee.

"Oh yea, I'm sure that's on his to-do list," Dean began, taking a sip of his healthy green tea. "Escape from prison, slice and kill the first female vic I see, send her heart to the detective, then, umm. Oh yeah, turn myself in." The humor was turning darker, a survival skill.

I thought about the viciously smug look Mules had on his face in court when he admitted to killing twenty women. When the district attorney asked about the other three, Mules simply replied, "If three baffles you, then you will be dumbfounded by those yet to come."

Today, I was reminded why Mules seemed to be so confident in his work. I finished my lunch and sat back with my glass of soda in hand.

"What in the world," Dean questioned when the door opened, ringing the bell and drawing all attention to who came in.

A group of youth casually sauntered in, coolly acting as though they weren't colorful in order to draw attention. It was the invasion of the little gnome dolls, the trolls my daughter had been so fond of. Each had a different bright color of hair. One of them had spikes that were each a different color. I wondered if this kind of creativity extended to school work.

Perry E. Zenon

I immediately thought about my statement to Eve-Marie at breakfast this morning.

"Don't even ask," I laughed, choking through my drink as we made eye contact.

"OK, enough levity. Back down to earth. Let's go catch the bad guy." And Dean, hitting his last slug of tea, rose in a dark, large, imposing, tight mass from the table.

I reached into my back pocket, extracted my wallet, and removed a five and ten dollar bill, enough to cover both of our meals and more than a twenty percent tip. I placed it all on the table.

Although we were supposed to leave the plates on the table, on our way out the door we took them over to the kitchen area. Gloria was coming to retrieve them anyway.

We did this so she wouldn't always insist that the meal was on the house and she can't see the table in the back with money on it before we leave. The eatery's kindness made us especially interested in its protection; we drove by it more carefully than most other places.

"You boys put those down right now," Gloria ordered as she lightly slapped us with the edge of the towel she used to wipe off the tables. "How many times I have to tell y'all to just leave them be?"

"You're going to have to keep tellin' us, ma'am," Dean slightly scolded her back.

"And, as always, the food was delicious," I added as we headed for the door.

Hearts

"Y'all be takin' care now," the Creole cautioned as she carried the plates to the kitchen.

It was nice. She meant it.

*****

The primary reasoning for an investigation is to locate and preserve identified evidence for theory building, arrest, prosecution, and conviction. She took pride in performing these skills scrupuously.

Unlike some of the investigators who carried their equipment in the trunk of their car, Detective Knowles preferred to drive what I referred to as the silver bullet. The silver van came to an abrupt stop next to a black-and-white and the doors opened, letting the detective free to roam the world.

Regular patrol was already at the scene after responding to the 10-38. The apartment where the incident was located was easy to spot by following the trail of uniforms going in and out the door that stood open. The living room was poorly furnished with things only tenants would consider to be of necessity.

On the sofa sat two officers who appeared to be questioning a child wrapped in a blanket. Realizing the detectives were now present, the officer not actively asking questions observed.

"Detective, this be the only member of the family who survived," indicating the burrito waif of a boy on the sofa. "And if you follow me, I will show you where the bodies are."

Perry E. Zenon

The officer weaved around the others who swarmed the house heading to the master bedroom. Lying on the floor were three bodies that had been covered to prevent what evidence that may lie around them from being tampered with. Bloodstained footprints were indicated for evidence with white cards with black numbers on them.

"They all were stabbed to death except for the little boy. From the blood on his clothes and the prints in the room, he came in after they were stabbed."

"Who made the call?" asked Knowles.

"The older son from the apartment below. We have him there if you want to question him."

"You mean to tell me he hasn't been questioned?" Xavier, the male detective, blurted.

"I'll question him and how about you go sit in on the boy's interview."

"But first, I think there is something I found a little odd."

"Which is?"

"The tenant informed us that the door was hooked when he came over, and there doesn't seem to be any sign of forced entry."

Chapter 6

We got back to the precinct and saw that Rogers had finished his previous analysis and placed the report of his findings on the desk. But it was Dean's desk instead of mine. That was unusual.

"Boy, Rogers sure did this one quick," Dean said as he picked up the report and began to read it.

I tried to remember the last time anyone gave a report directly to Dean, our team's secondary man.

As his face slowly began to distort, something apparently became very wrong, and I rapidly felt cold. An ice cube feeling stuck in my throat.

I knew something was out of whack.

Perry E. Zenon

The more he read, the quieter the room seemed to become.

My legs didn't want to support my weight any longer and I had to sit down.

I could sense my newly erratic heart as Dean looked at me in immobilized shock; and with compassion he quietly handed me the report, saying, "The testing indicates that the heart belonged to Heather Callow."

This was absolutely insane.

Eighteen months ago, a body was found by a runner while I was in Baton Rouge giving a briefing on crime scene investigation. I was only gone for the duration of the briefing and the time it took to drive there and back.

Upon returning to the office, I noticed a report on Dean's desk. I knew it had to be another victim from the series of murders we were investigating, so I filled myself in by reading the report.

There have only been two times in my life when time did not move. The first was when I met my Heather at a party. This day, eighteen months ago, was the last. The murder that morning, when I was out of town and not there for my love, was my Heather. And I had just objectively wanted an objective update, not my life shattered.

The room seemed to spin. I fought to keep it from fogging out.

Today, as I read my wife's name, Dean softly reminded me we already knew that she had fallen victim to the notorious serial murderer who was taking the hearts of his victims. Heather's heart was one of the

Hearts

three that we never found. I always assumed that he chose hearts at random to keep as his souvenir trophy.

Because of technicalities and expediency for the legal system, Mules was only convicted with seventeen of the twenty charges of murder. My wife was one of the six for whom he wasn't credited.

I guess this was just his way of telling me for sure that he was responsible for the death of my wife. I simultaneously wanted to vomit, to scream uncontrollably, and to, as a natural response, find him and kill him.

Although I had an aggravated reason to personally encourage and participate in his demise, my job was to be dispassionate so that emotions don't cloud my intellectual reach.

My ears felt as if I'd been dropped into the fog vacuum.

My precious piece of chocolate, my Heather now was gone from me for many months. Finally, I'm usually not overtly angry, although I'll admit it simmers.

She will never be gone from my heart, soul and very being, although I have accepted that she has gone home. I guess there is still a remnant of her old Baptist and our newer, combined Catholicism in me. But not much.

"We will catch him again," Dean reassured as the phone began to ring.

I picked up the phone and the silence from the other end had an odd, hollow sense about it.

"Detective Callow."

My mouth felt as if I had eaten a whole bag of cotton, and the words I wanted to say were caught in my throat.

Perry E. Zenon

I swallowed hard to get them and my physiological reaction down.

"Something kept me from telling you three years ago that I killed your wife," the mechanical voice continued.

If it weren't for the hollowness and the buzz in the active receiver, I would have hung up, assuming that he was no longer there.

"The heart in the box is hers."

I was awestricken by the arrogance of his reminding me of this.

"You have no response? No question? No fit of emotion? You already read the report, didn't you? I wanted to enjoy telling you myself."

My diaphragm stopped working and my breath seemed to abruptly stop. My knuckles tensed to red as I clutched the phone tighter. Despite the coolness in the room, I was sweating profusely, almost woozy with enragement.

"Well, understand this romantic thought. She gave her heart to you, now her heart is forever yours."

A chill of insurmountable proportions overcame me. I was unknowingly taking deep, deep breaths to get enough oxygen to survive.

"You sick son of a..."

The silencing of the buzz cut me off as I began screaming pointed, personal obscenities.

I hung up the receiver, stared without seeing it, and finally collapsed back in my chair with a cavernous sigh.

"That wasn't who I think it is?"

Hearts

Grimly, "Have them find out where that call originated."

"OK, but I don't think he's taking you putting him in the joint lightly." Dean was trying to joke as he walked to his desk and picked up the phone.

*****

He sat patiently in his sedan, waiting for the traffic to allow him an opportunity to exit Interstate Ten. Willy Simmering tapped the steering wheel while listening to Kirk Franklin's "Lovely Day."

The soft melody relaxed his mind, giving him control of his anger while decreasing the number of potential victim motorists of road rage.

He took the off-ramp down to the boulevard below while the CD player randomly selected another track from the disk. He flipped open his cellular phone and adjusted the earpiece to his ear.

"Liz."

Willy spoke into the phone just loud enough for the microphone to pick up his voice. The phone began to dial the memory number that corresponded to the name that was spoken.

With no answer at the number, Willy closed the phone and pulled into the driveway of his tract home.

He scooped the mail from the box, thumbed through it for anything of importance, then walked to the door.

The porch light automatically came on as he approached the door, illuminating a package sitting there.

Perry E. Zenon

Satisfied that all he had received was junk mail, he unlocked the door and then stooped down to pick up the box. He went inside and placed the mail on the coffee table.

He sighed upon realizing that, again, nothing was taken out for dinner. Opening the refrigerator, he spotted the sad container of previously canned spaghetti left over from the night before.

Before getting a plate out of the cupboard, Willy automatically whisked the remote off the counter and switched the TV to local news. The male announcer was gravely announcing the finding of a body whom police said was one the inmates who escaped from the penitentiary bus over the weekend.

The usually perky, blonde female counterpart looked on as she supported her counterpart with seriousness.

"Like I said, He will see to it that justice is served!" Willy exclaimed, talking to himself about his old acquaintances, the detectives.

Willy placed his plate in the microwave, and after placing a napkin over it to keep the sauce from getting all over, he set the timer and grabbed a canned drink from the `fridge.

While waiting, he remembered the package. Willy went into the living room. Setting the can on the table, he picked up the box and checked the name before he opened it, politely ensuring that he didn't open his wife's package.

He placed the box back on the table, took a cool sip of his drink, and then used a pen to break through the

Hearts

tape on the box. Upon opening the box he reached underneath the bubble wrap and pulled out a bag.

"Holy...," he gasped, dropping the bag to the floor while he sprung to his feet.

Willy rushed to the cordless phone that sat in its cradle next to the sofa and disbelievingly stared in the direction of the box. Urgently and sloppily he turned on the phone and began to dial.

"911, may I help you," said the voice on the other end.

Although his voice was quaking, Willy, almost sobbing, blurted to the dispatch operator that he just opened a box.

"It contains something that appears to be a heart, maybe a human heart, man."

*****

The sun began to retire for the night, allowing his counterpart room to reign until he was ready to take over his territory and command the sky again.

While the change of luminous command was under way, three men stood on the edge of an empty pool looking at Mules' former chain-mate who had been carelessly thrown into the pool by the drain, causing him to blaspheme in pain when his body came into contact with the cement.

"You!" Larry Mules tapped his hired assassin who stood on his right. "Get down there, take the chair and chain him to it, and then secure the chair to the drain."

Larry Mules believed in earning your wages and was

Perry E. Zenon

insistent on his hired help earning every penny he agreed
to pay them.

"I thought you said our job was to get you off the bus?" Muscles stated while climbing into the pool as ordered.

"How right you are, you are free to go." Mules pointed to the gate indicating the way to exit.

"Oh, why aren't we leaving, then?"

Muscles swallowed the insult and silently descended the ladder in the pool with his right hand on the railing, chair under his left arm, and began to walk to the middle.

"That's right, because you haven't been paid," Mules taunted him.

"Hey, man," Mitch strangled out a yell to Mules as he staggered to his feet.

"You don't have to kill me. I won't tell no one where y'all go."

"Dear boy," Mules uttered, walking around the edge of the pool toward Mitch. "If I wanted to ensure you wouldn't speak of my whereabouts, I would simply shoot you in your face."

"Then what this `bout? Man, I ain't done you nothin'," Mitch began to whine.

Mitch backed away from Muscles until his back was against the wall.

"Whoever said I'm doing anything to get back at you, or that I even care about you enough to consider punishing." Mules was now standing on the edge above him, noncommittally looking down on Mitch with glee.

Hearts

Muscles placed the chair over the drain and moved in towards Mitch with his arms spread, trying to block all avenues of escape.

"No, Boy, you just a pawn in this game and it's time that I made my move."

Mitch's screams for compassion seemed to please his tormenter as he agilely left the pool going to the house, leaving his crew outside in the fresh air where the moon bathed them in luminosity as they tied their bait to the chair.

Perry E. Zenon

Chapter 7

The crowd that eagerly drew almost all around the house at the end of the cul-de-sac seemed to be morbidly attracted by the lure of the red and blue beacons of the police cruisers. People parted to allow passage of my sedan. I parked behind the squad car and switched off the portable Rawls light that sat on my dash and we exited the vehicle.

"I haven't heard anything 'bout old Willy since the accident," Dean mentioned as he closed the door.

After our high school days, Willy Simmering played football for Grambling State University where he was immediately drafted into the pros. During the first season, he was in a car accident that placed him in a coma for three months. When he came through, he wasn't playing football anymore.

"Yes, it has been a long time since he has been the focus of the sports column in the Times Picayune."

We entered the house and immediately went to the back where the voices were. Sitting in a chair by a wall was the former adolescent football star with his head hung low. A uniformed police officer was questioning him and paused as we passed through the archway.

"Sir, would you like me to update you on the situation?" The officer spoke to us as he turned his gaze away from Willy.

"No, not now. Thanks."

I began to tour the modest home, ensuring not to travel too far so that the conversation could still be heard. It never hurts to compare story versions.

"Is this it?" Dean asked, referring to a small brown box that sat on the coffee table.

Willy said, "Yes," allowing his head to again fall helplessly into his cradling hands.

Something occurred to me and I began to become gratingly uneasy. It wasn't uncommon for an athlete to purchase a house, especially an athlete whose people never owned one, but I clearly remembered that Willy purchased this particular house because after they married, his wife insisted they would start a family.

"Is the missus home?" I casually approached, walking towards the chair that he had sunk deeply into.

As he lifted his head, I could see that this was also his question, and I almost regretted asking it. A tear slipped down his face to under his chin and he was unable to answer.

The phone rang.

The ringing resonated through and off the walls, making its sound part of the house. No one moved. No one acknowledged the fact that a phone existed or that it was ringing.

"Would you like me to get it?" Dean never was one who could endure silence.

Willy nodded yes dumbly.

Dean walked towards the kitchen where the ringing was originating, retrieved a still ringing cordless phone and handed it to Willy.

*****

It stank from the rancid mixture of sweat and blood being confined in an area that lacked proper ventilation. The room was filled with a soft buzz from the nearby computer and there was a slight tapping as the call was being scrambled. The telemarketer for death was sitting with headset on, calling to notify those who the recently deceased were survived by.

"She gave you her heart, and her heart is yours forever," the low voice spoke into the microphone, sending this tad bit of information through the voice manipulator.

After brutally "explaining" to Willy that his wife was an adulterous woman, the telemarketer heard Detective Callow's voice and asked to speak to him.

Perry E. Zenon

"Well, I'm sure a smart detective like you has already figured out that the heartless stiff from earlier today is Willy's precious Elizabeth. Dear, dear Mr. Detective, you can be so touchy at times. I expected you to be easier to talk to, being a free man now and all."

The line was disconnected.

*****

We headed out of the neighborhood in the car, holding the only apparent available evidence from the Simmering residence. My cell phone rang. I pulled the vehicle over

"Detective Callow," I harshly snarled into the tiny phone receiver.

"If you are looking for my shackle mate, Detective, he can be found at the bottom of a pool." I listened. "He is currently alive, I assure you, but if you don't find him soon he will surely drown."

I always carried a little spiral pad in which I wrote all salient information that a case needed. I was a bit disoriented, not realizing that Mules had my private cell number; I pulled out my pad from my shirt but my pen eluded me. I elbowed Dean, whose attention was fixed on me already, and I frantically motioned for him to hand me his pen.

"Check thirty-eight fifty-two Cypress Street," Mules gloated before ending the call.

I entered the address into our auto's computer database to obtain the direct route to the house and pulled the vehicle onto the road again. Making a right, instead of the left out of the neighborhood as I would have done if I were retracing our way in there, I flipped the switch and let the sirens wail.

"Who was that and what is this?" Dean was looking at the address that blinked on the screen.

"Mules. He told me where we can get the guy who was shackled to him. We might be lookin' at clues." We were both yelling.

"Why didn't he tell you that when we were at Willy's place and you were on the phone with him? Scumbag game player."

Dean was getting worked up, and I shrugged my shoulders to his rhetorical question, but I was wondering the same.

Our screaming vehicle came to a dead stop in the neighborhood. The lights and cautionary siren brought watchers to their window and an elderly lady stepped outside when we stopped in front of her house.

"What is wrong, officer?" She hobbled to us with a seemingly displaced hip. She walked along the neat walkway with some difficulty as we disobeyed her pleading sign to stay off the grass.

"We need to see your pool," Dean demanded, already in route to the rear of the house.

"Wait, I don't have no pool." She seemed amazed as Dean continued behind the house, persistent in seeing the pool she wasn't aware she had.

"What is your name?" I asked her, taking out the pad and pencil to record the information

Perry E. Zenon

"My name, Officer, is Mrs. Hood, Teala Hood. This," she pointed behind her with rising indignation, "be my house, so I would certainly know if there be a pool."

Teala was definitely upset that Dean went looking behind the house after she said she did not own a pool.

"There's no pool back there," Dean informed me of this, disappointed.

"I already said that!" Teala screeched, obviously agitated. "That's the problem with cops today, you don't listen and quick to accuse. Is it hard to believe that I knew that already, huh?" Her pitch rose.

"Well, when we received a call giving your address, our first thought was to protect you and we must ensure public safety," said Dean patiently.

"Call? I never called you," Teala shrieked.

"I never said you did." Between her voice and the disappointment, Dean's patience was rapidly wearing thin.

"Mrs. Hood." I calmly and politely stepped in, moving Dean behind me.

"We just received a call from a man who told us that we should check the pool at this address for a man who just escaped from prison. So we were obligated to follow through with the lead."

"Well," she calmed down, then gained momentum again, "So, I'm the old lady and don't know where you need to look; but maybe next time you should check to see if there is a pool before you go looking for it." Her vocal inflection changed to the upswing of haughtiness.

"We will keep that in mind."

"Anything else I can help you with?"

Hearts

"No, but you have been a great help," with controlled steadiness.

"I'm sure. Well if you be excusing me." Mrs. Teala Hood repeated a rote nicety before slowly walking back toward the house on her neatly placed pebble walkway, leaving us standing on her lawn.

*****

"Man I just don't have time for them birds tonight."

Because he lived only four blocks from the precinct, Dean would walk to work on those rare occasions when he actually heard "the birds signing" as he so elegantly put it.

"You know I have no problem taking you home, or picking you up for that matter."

"Oh, I know. But you don't get in as early as I like."

Dean's time in the military had him accustomed to going to bed late and waking early. He denies it, but I'm sure he even works out before coming to work and often worked out on precinct equipment.

I pulled up to the curb next to the walkway.

"I'll catch ya' tomorrow then."

"All right. Tell that godchild of mine I said hello and that we will have to do something soon. Maybe catch that new Christian play `He say, she say, but what does God say?' or whatever."

I waited till he was inside before I drove off and headed home.

"I put you a plate in the microwave."

Perry E. Zenon

Eve-Marie had already eaten and the mess I'm sure she created while cooking had already been cleaned. She sat in the living room watching television.

"Thank you, what you cooked?"

"Your favorite, shrimp stir-fry."

It wasn't my favorite meal, I just liked Heather's better than anyone else's. I never had the heart to tell my daughter this, though.

I snatched the plate out of the microwave without warming it up and opened the fridge for something to drink.

"I made you some Kool Aid too."

"OK. What do you need and how much is it going to cost me in the long run?"

One thing Eve-Marie learned from her mother was to butter me up with food to get what she wanted.

"I didn't say I wanted anything."

Her inability to lie came from me.

"I just know how much you like stir-fry and cherry Kool Aid."

I walked out of the kitchen with plate and cup in hand and saw that she had already set up a TV tray for me.

"You forget what it is I do for a living."

"Well, there is this party."

"Ahh, a party. The answer is no."

"But, Daddy."

I acted as though I were ignoring her and standing firm on my decision. She sat where I could see her and began to pout, another of Heather's contributions.

"When and where?"

"Julie's house on her birthday this weekend."

Hearts

"I didn't say you can go yet, you're still supposed to be pouting."

"Please."

"Only if you finish your school work and her parents are there the whole time."

I worried too much - perhaps.

"Thank you, thank you."

But with Heather being taken from me and Mules being out once again, I wasn't ready to put anything on faith; not a characteristic of cops, anyway.

Perry E. Zenon

Tuesday

"What shall we then say to these
things?
If God be for us, who can be
against us?"

Romans 8:31

Perry E. Zenon

Chapter 8

My body searched for the source of the noise that interrupted my dream state. I reached over to the nightstand. Opening the drawer, I extracted my Berretta. Heather hated it being there. I inserted the clip. I heard a thud as something fell onto the linoleum floor in the kitchen and I eased out of bed, holding my elevated pistol, both hands locked, to the side.

I slowly opened the door, relieved that the door didn't squeak. Easing down the hall past Eve-Marie's door, I followed my weapon that was in readiness and stopped at the corner to listen. Hearing no sound, I moved around the wall into the living room, performing a quick scan with my eyes following the tracks of my gun, as I made my way into the kitchen.

Perry E. Zenon

"Drop your weapon or I'll gut her like the pig you are."

Larry Mules held a knife inches from the chest of my baby girl and I reluctantly placed my weapon on the floor. Eve-Marie turned her head and looked at me with terror from the table she was lying upon.

A tear wanted to fall from my eye and roll down my cheek.

"This is between me and you. How `bout you let her go and take me instead?"

I wanted to kill him more than ever, with an intensity of passion almost unknown to me before. If he gave me the slightest opportunity, I would.

"No, Detective Callow, I don't want you to take her place, I want you to watch."

He raised the knife about to strike.

"No!" My daughter's and my deep, intense, piercing shrieks occurred at the same time.

I automatically jumped forward, frantically trying to stop him before he brought the blade down but arrived only in time to watch my daughter's twisted little caramel face as the blade broke through her skin.

I sprang up in the bed, heart pounding against my chest. Drying my face, I grabbed the pistol from the nightstand, inserting the clip in one movement. I not so cautiously eased to the kitchen to ease my distressed mind.

Within seconds, I arrived at Eve-Marie's door; I looked in and released a strangled sigh upon seeing her lying peacefully in bed.

Hearts

I checked my watch, realizing that it was still early in the morning. Time to get some more sleep, now that I finally could with the most horrific dream of my life broken.

*****

At daybreak, a lone van sat in the parking area by the lake with the ignition running and the lights turned off. The rear doors gaped open.

After tossing a wad of trash bags and tape into the cargo hold, the driver slammed the doors and returned to the driver's seat.

With the ignition shifted into drive, the lights came on and the van pulled away as the person left behind lay on the cold ground, blankly gazing after it.

Her tangled hair waved in the slight breeze, following the track of the person responsible for freeing her from a life of adultery.

Dena Guidry was positioned silently, as if she had willingly planned a day of relaxation and gazing at the runners and walkers that would arrive soon.

Body still, face frozen in distortion from the heart-capturing ordeal responsible for her current condition, she waited.

*****

I positioned myself back in my comfortably worn chair, trying to engage in peace of mind in the mix of

Perry E. Zenon

mild cacophony as the other detectives scurried about with their assignments.

"You know this is impossible," Detective Cain Xavier almost whined as he entered the office with Jade following behind him.

"Impossible? You think everything is impossible, Cain. If we relied on your negativity as fact, we wouldn't get anywhere, ever. We'd just get on the slide and go all the way to the bottom." Adding emphasis, her graceful arm and hand swooped out then turned up like a ballet dancer's pose.

I watched Jade flowing through the room, remembering the first time she walked into the office after Chief announced a new homicide detective.

It wasn't long before the veterans, ignoring the warnings of Title VII's bill that clarifies equal opportunity, began insinuations that she should be in a kitchen where women belong. She probably also should have been more appropriately attired without shoes and in "that" condition. Actually, she looked great.

"Hey...," Jade started, walking over toward me.

Startled, I reflexively jerked my head a bit when she was suddenly within inches of my face.

"Hey, what are you staring at?" Jade questioned, placing her folder on my desk.

"I was just thinking..." I couldn't find anything to say without giving the wrong impression so I decided to evade the question.

"What is this?" I tapped the folder that she had placed on my desk.

Hearts

"This is the jacket from the case I've been assigned to. I remembered that case you had with the little boy and thought you might be able to help."

Before I began having hearts delivered to me on a timely basis, I had arrived on a double homicide and the murderer turned out to be a ten-year-old boy.

I picked up the folder and begin reading through it as a diversion to the thoughts piling up in my head. Jade and Cain's case involved a family unit of four who were murdered except for the youngest son, who managed to survive.

"The boy is the only suspect I have; I just don't know how to go about questioning a grieving, shocked child to discern if he killed his family or not, even if he was the last person known to see them alive."

I gave her advice on the possibilities, hoping she could benefit from my mistakes. That was as long as I could attend to something besides my own need to solve a case. I heard Dean's sonorous voice.

"I'm tired of this!"

"What's up with you?" I asked, getting up and going around to the other side of his desk to sit on the end.

"This case is doggin' me. It could develop into bloody insanity, bro."

I personally didn't consider Dean to be sane, but then again, who am I to determine sanity.

Sane or not, this was the first time a case had him acting differently. The ordeal was an intimate experience for us. We may have a long haul in this case and it's only been a day since we had to reopen a jacket whose closure we celebrated a few months ago.

Perry E. Zenon

"Dean, just..." The ringing of my phone derailed my train of thought. "Hold on a minute."

I flipped open my phone and placed it to my ear. "Detective..."

Sarcastically, "Why do you state who you are when I just called your number?"

The sickening feeling returned. The rage flared as the voice of Larry Mules harassed my ear. Had I not been convinced it would cause permanent damage, I would have dropped the phone and scorched my ear against further auditory input.

"I realized that the address wasn't correct when I was home, but I'm sure it's something like it," playfully ugly.

I replayed in my mind the precise moment when I had Mules at gunpoint, wanting to choose this time to pull the trigger. But Heather's sweet, warning face entered into my mind and my mood was lightened.

"Forgive me for this, but the poor boy will drown if you don't find him soon."

I thought about chasing Mules' game for the third time today, but not for long. I just couldn't handle another elderly, shrieking female again, and my partner also needed to give it a rest.

"You up for some Cheesecake Bistro?" I asked the man whom I know wouldn't give up a chance to eat--especially healthy food with milk in it.

"Hey bro', that's just what I might need. Let's give it a shot," Dean replied, in his belief that food solves everything.

Hearts

Fifteen minutes later, we turned off at the famous Bistro after passing miles of street car lines on St. Charles Avenue, and found a parking space near the patio tables. I opened the heavy, European door, engulfed by the savory aroma of steak and Alfredo sauce. Almost immediately, our hostess tried to seat us at one of the booths by the window. We sought a less obvious place in the back, so we could see what was happening and our backs would be protected.

"Hi, my name is Tracey and I will be your server for today," she perked. "Oh and I think you officers would love today's special."

At her cue, we made mental room for the shrimp almandine and salad.

This enticing lady standing by our table's personality seemed to be an escort to the vivacious ambiance. We ordered our food and pretended to relax, working on recapturing any sanity that the morning had already taken by storm.

Shrimp almandine is bite-sized shrimp, fried in a spicy batter, covered in an almond sauce, and sprinkled with almond slices. It costs a little over ten bucks. We had enough for both of us and Dean also ordered the shrimp, crab and avocado salad, a terrific mixture of romaine lettuce and other greens with more shrimp boiled, tomatoes, red onions, black olives, and finally, egg, dressed with a house dressing and covered with fried crab and avocado, costing about thirteen bucks. This feast carries one through to next day's breakfast.

Perry E. Zenon

"So, how has my godchild been? I haven't seen her in a few weeks," said my good friend Dean. My parents' only son, me, married an only child, Heather, and when it came to the important decision for godparents of baby Eve-Marie, we asked Dean if he would accept the loving responsibilities that came with the title. So far he has not reneged on his agreement.

"She's good. I think she's trying to do too much though."

"What do you mean?"

"Well on top of school `till now, and being a teenager she's been studying the Bible and trying to fill her mother's shoes. And, she needs to get back into summer sports."

Tracey returned, the vivacious waitress in a European-ambiance apron.

"Here we go, guys, and let me know if you need anything."

"Hey, who called before we left?"

"Called?" I couldn't put off eating the shrimp any longer. "Oh, it was my buddy Mules."

"It's funny how you say a murderer called you in the same text someone would say their spouse called." Dean tossed a shrimp into his mouth. "It's just not that common."

"Well, he just wanted to tell me about the other prisoner and the pool."

"Didn't he do that yesterday?"

"I guess he can't keep them organized," I joked.

Hearts

"Enough about that noise," Dean began switching gears, "you know I love you and I wouldn't steer you wrong, right, bro?"

When depending on another person to watch your back as you watch theirs for nine years, you ultimately develop a level of trust.

"Yes, of course I know that." I looked at Dean worriedly. "Where you goin' with this?"

"Well," Dean picked up his cup of tea and took a sip, then replaced it on the table. "I think you should move on and start dating."

"You..."

"Now before you object, let me finish. You have to stop blaming God for what happened."

Dean Smith doesn't sugarcoat.

He stopped talking, but I knew he wasn't finished so I ate the shrimp while waiting for him to finish his statement.

"It's not the trials and tribulations we endure that shape us into the person He wants us to be, it's what we take from them. You know, making lemonade when you're stuck with lemons."

I couldn't argue with him, so instead I sat there and reflected on the reality of his statement.

"There are women out there and I think you should give them a chance," my friend continued.

"Don't you mean a woman?" I inquired.

"No, I meant what I said and since you brought her up, yes, I think she should be considered."

"I love my wife, dead or not." It was a firm but almost petulant response.

Perry E. Zenon

"I know you love her and I'm not suggesting you
stop loving her either. I just think that you need to have
a life, and in time maybe you can learn to love someone
else as well. You and I have a certain type of deep love,
you and I love Eve-Marie, love can be different and
there can be more than one."

"What about your red bombshell Loretta?" I teased.

"You are not responding appropriately to a grave
moment," Dean intoned.

"Look, just because it's you--and yes, we are
brothers, I have listened. If you are making good points,
it will come to me when I'm ready, OK?"

I re-concluded, "OK?" This was the farthest I'd ever
come toward change and he knew it.

Satisfied and sort of relieved, he nodded and got back
to his tea and there was a healthy silence between us for
a moment or two.

We left the restaurant with our stomachs full, with
appetites satisfied and a to-go box in our hands.

Dean insisted that going to Cheesecake Bistro and
not getting cheesecake is like going to a steak house and
not ordering a steak.

Chapter 9

Robert opened the door to his home to leave for work, and the heat from the sun-baked day collided with the air-conditioned environment he was leaving. The man moved carefully, closing and locking the door behind him. Moving toward his vehicle, he first stopped to pick up a small brown wrapped carton by his mailbox that wasn't there before. Entering the car, he tossed it on the passenger seat before settling in behind the wheel of his Explorer.

He rolled down all four windows to let out the contained stagnant, hot and humid air and waved to Mrs. Lee next door as he checked to make sure he had everything for work.

Perry E. Zenon

Once in motion, Robert, a careful overachiever by nature, could catch every red light, travel below the posted speed limit on the expressway, this after being held up in traffic on the Crescent City Connection, and still arrive to work ahead of schedule. Because he set the clocks in his house ten minutes fast, Robert would still leave early enough to allow for unforeseeable mishaps, giving him an hour to make a trip which required only twenty minutes.

Robert was a planner.

Calmly sitting in traffic over the Mississippi River, Robert remembered the package and briefly stared at it. Trying to identify the contents without actually opening it, Robert grasped the box with his thumb and forefinger and held it to his ear. He shook it back and forth as one would with a nicely wrapped gift in white paper with reindeer scenes printed all over.

He noticed the traffic begin to move, gave up on his tentative art of seeing through boxes, and ripped it open with the same hand. He took his foot off the brake pedal, briefly looking away from the road ahead. Then, ensuring that he wouldn't hit cars in front of him, he again quickly attended to the box in his lap. He worked at opening it with his right hand. When he caught another moment, Robert withdrew the prize--a quart size, ziplocked bag.

Although traffic was not moving at a high rate of speed, when he saw the contents of the bag, a slight screech was heard from the tires as they came to a brusque stop.

Hearts

The vehicle's momentum wiggled a little bit further.

He removed the ziplocked bag, its gory contents coldly intact.

*****

With no rigidly established lunch time or duration, police personnel in the field had to be adults and mostly make their own decisions on when and where to eat. What surprised me is that we all took our lunches on or around the same time, probably due to our bodies being trained from the age of five when we begin school, and we ate lunch between eleven and one.

It wasn't quite one yet; the office seemed to be frozen in the state we had left it. As Dean and I entered our office, it thawed.

"Good, you're here," sang a happy, relieved voice coming through the door that joined our homicide office with the main office.

It was Skip Landers, a baby-faced boy in blue who made the force because his doting father had important people owing him one.

"I think you should talk to this gentleman."

Following Skip was a nervous fellow wearing Wranglers perhaps two sizes too small, and a swell Western, partially undone button-down shirt to complete the ensemble. The only part of his overall outfit I related to was the familiar, small brown box.

"I found this thing outside my house," he shakily stated, extending the box for one of us to take.

Perry E. Zenon

"What is your name?" I inquired, still leaving him holding the prize in his shaking hand.

"My name is Robert Guidry and I'm late for work."

*****

A hard-working figure called the number that was next to Robert Guidry's name on the scrap of paper. The work was being done while sitting in the murk and using a computer which alters the voice and scrambles the location of the call. It was getting a good workout lately.

After two hours in the room, the figure again became accustomed to the stench. The ringing of the phone being called sang through the speakers and seemed to bounce off the walls in an endless tone like one long ring. On the fourth ring, the answering machine answered.

"You have reached the Guidry residence. We are not available at the time. Feel free to call our cell phone at..."

Next to the house number the cellular phone number was written, the line was reset, and the new number dialed.

*****

There was no need to keep a shaken Robert here for more questioning than he could handle when we knew that, as with Willy, Robert had no idea why he now was the new intermediate owner of a used blood pumping station.

Hearts

After we talked and we searched for any information he could unwittingly have, he was leaving through the door he entered. He stopped and retrieved a phone from his pocket.

"Hello!"

The earpiece volume was high enough that I could hear the mechanical voice a foot away.

"When a person gives their heart to someone..."

I pointed and mouthed to Dean, "That's him."

The mechanical voice had a robotic, scrambled tone to it. With every word, another hair pricked on end.

"It is only that person's and no one can take it from them," the robot sneered. "She's stopped giving your heart away, thanks to me. You now have her heart in your hands forever."

I remembered the personalized message that accompanied the perp's trophy belonging to my wife, and I was instantly there, projecting my own pain, flushed with rage. Understandably, the department is very uncomfortable having detectives working cases that personally involve them, which is why my veneer of normalcy was so carefully controlled. I wanted this guy. Once wasn't enough.

I watched Robert's excruciatingly contorted face as he received this terrible news. I'm sure the contortion could be seen in my face when he handed me the phone. I sure felt it.

"This is Detective Callow, who's this?"

"Hello, Detective."

Perry E. Zenon

I heard the static from the calls prior, confirming my previous assumption of the cause of the buzz and also the receiver's hollow sound.

"The poor, lonely cowboy, he actually believed that a girl of her magnitude could be faithful to herself, let alone someone else."

Listening to this vicious, self-proclaimed judger of moral rights, I regretted not putting a bullet in his head when I had the chance. I felt certain Heather looking down on me would understand.

"Do you have something to write on? I think you might find this to be helpful."

I listened and wrote down the location that was given for the heartless body and remembered the pool.

"So, is there nobody at this address like there wasn't any pool at the last?"

Silence. "I never said anything about a pool last time. Last time we spoke, I advised you to not let people get to you." The retort was designed to be clever.

I thought for a minute, searching for the conversation in Willy's living room.

"Speaking of last time, try not to get so bent when you're talking to the `first to arrive'. You really should play nice." Then, nothing.

I stared at the words "call disconnected" on the screen and my mind replayed the events leading up to today.

Something was so unbalanced.

Perhaps lots of somethings, and Dean and I hadn't moved into any additions to a new theory either. I couldn't figure out exactly what I was sensing.

Hearts

Gratefully, it occurred to me as I handed Robert his cell phone.

"Mules didn't use an encryption device when he called my cell phone," I firmly related, puzzled.

"Why would he?" Dean asked. "He knows you already know his identity." He sounded like a mentally exhausted, sarcastic cop.

I briefly got back to Robert.

"You get to work now, or take the day off and find someone to talk to. Take care of yourself, please, and we'll meet with you later,"

I went to the door, saying, "Detective Smith, we got to go."

Perry E. Zenon

Chapter 10

Late May rain was hovering in the air's seventy-seven percent humidity. That, combined with the temperature, brought an approximate eighty-nine degree heat equivalent. Already. By late June, July there would be heat warnings. Today, daytime background music chirped from a blue bird as if it were the most perfect day, although perhaps a bit muggy.

We called ahead and then raced to the crime scene past the shrimp lots, the marketplaces featuring little stands with entrepreneurs selling seafood. The only reason we noticed this time was to take care that our screaming vehicle avoided the uninterested hordes of buyers. Sometimes the community we loved and protected did little to help us in return.

Before we could arrive, the area was thankfully swarming with uniforms trying to keep the reporters out of the area and the crime scene untouched.

Dean and I walked under the yellow tape, displaying our IDs to satisfy any officers who could be concerned that we didn't belong.

"Oh here we go again," I half whispered to Dean as I saw the unkempt, mousy blonde officer from yesterday assertively heading in our direction.

"Can you believe this?" I admit her first question invoked a hateful side of me that I was reluctant to openly expose prior to altogether losing it.

"Who would'uh think this would happen again," she chortled. "Beales, remember?"

I'm not sure what bothered me more: her appearance, questions, demeanor, or her overzealous, pleased attitude at a murder scene.

She was sure an amateur, the kind of girl-woman unusual for the careful standards of the force.

Dean looked at her, then at the expression on my face and smirked, just to himself this time. I think she was really rubbing his emotions the wrong way too.

I left smirking Dean with the dippity officer while I performed the duties detectives are paid to perform. Just as with Mrs. Simmering, this parallel site wasn't a murder location but the place chosen for the body to be found, and judging from the amount of rigor mortis that had already set in, it was evident her death wasn't recent. I took pictures of the area as it was found and instructed the field guys to pack her up.

"Are you two finished?" I returned to Dean.

"Yes," Dean began and walked over to me, pointing at his pad. "Beales was catching me up on information from the guy who found the body; he had to leave. I'll be getting his own report, though."

"Callow," Dean said as he tapped me with his pad. "What's wrong?" He was probing because I was on a different plane than ever before.

"I can almost put my finger on it." I stared at the cars passing by, trying to figure out the missing puzzle pieces. Sometimes when I just relax, the information flows into me.

I used to think that it was a "God thing." No more. And the information didn't readily flow either.

"Well someone has just been murdered." Beales was making gentle fun of my lack of humor.

"Okay, we can handle it from here," directed to the dippity, vacuous mousy being in front of us.

"Hey, I was just trying to make conversation, didn't mean to get under your skin," Beales pouted and walked away, out of earshot.

"That's it," I told Dean as I grabbed his arm.

"What's it, what are you talking about?"

"When we were analyzing the murder scene yesterday she was getting on my nerves."

"What's your point?"

I left Dean there, looking confused as I surveyed the area looking for Mules. I realized he had been watching us at the crime scenes.

Perry E. Zenon

Dean walked over to me. "Callow, what..."

"He's here."

"Who's here?" Smith asked because he didn't understand my determined exploration.

"Mules, he's here, I know it."

The only people who I could actually see were two uniforms getting into the patrol car and the coroner staff, and none of them was Mules.

Baffled, but respectfully, Dean asked, "How do you know?"

"Let's go, better to explain at the office."

*****

The rain broke through the accumulated humidity and fell, just as the door to the precinct was closing behind us. I morbidly thought about the potential of Mules' victims' bodies under a tree, getting wet, either being washed clean from their horror or becoming disrespectfully soggy.

"OK, what's going on?" We were officially at the office; Dean couldn't wait any longer.

"When Mules was taunting me on the phone, he mentioned to not let people get under my skin."

I spoke over my shoulder as I led him to the inner, more private office.

"And I hadn't made the connection until today; he couldn't know that Beales was getting to me unless he was watching."

"You think he was there," Dean inquired as he followed me into the office.

Hearts

"I don't know if he was there today, but he had to be there yesterday or he wouldn't have known."

"Who had to be where?" Xavier was walking by the open door; he interrupted and came in followed by his partner Jade. She entered too. She wasn't an intrusion.

We ignored Detective Xavier's question as if we didn't hear him.

"Oh by the way," Jade was talking to me. "Thanks for helping me with the case. Turns out the little boy didn't kill his people after all."

I turned an eye towards Jade, not sure to what she was referring to.

"My case, the slain family survived by the youngest son."

"Oh yeah, so what did happen?"

"The dad did it!" Xavier butted in.

"The dad? I thought the only one to survive was the boy?" Dean followed in behind Xavier.

"After further investigation and questioning, we discovered that in a fit of rage, the father killed the mother and when the son tried to stop him he was accidentally killed. Realizing what he had done, the father killed himself and the littlest boy hid the knife."

"Why'd he do a thing like that?" Dean gave voice to the same thing I was thinking.

"When we asked him, he said he didn't want anyone to know what his dad did."

"So next time, and we seem to presently not be able to prevent the next time, our priority will be finding Mules." Dean was continuing my train of thought, fully intoned with our case.

Perry E. Zenon

Giving voice to that name re-grabbed attention in the room as if they hadn't been witnesses to the foul organ I received. It seems, even though one `knows', there are different, gut levels of awareness.

"Callow, umm...you think Mules is doing this?" Jade wondered with worry in her voice.

"This is the deal." I sat on the edge of Xavier's desk in the detective room and they drew in closer.

"We all know Mules escaped Sunday."

"Yes," all concurred.

"And we all saw my, my, uh package."

"Who could forget that," Jade stated and Xavier vigorously shook his head in agreement.

"Well. Let me give y'all a rundown of the events after that," speaking to the two.

"We had a body of a girl. When we arrived, she had no heart and the first officer on the scene was a dippy-doodle, getting on my nerves."

"That's always," Xavier noted.

"Yeah I know, let me finish. When we got back to the office we get the report, finding that my package that morning was the heart of my wife."

"Oh no!" Jade's pain for me was palpable as she weakly sat down in the chair.

"Do you think you should be working this case?" Xavier was rightfully worried it could become more personal than I, or anyone, would be or should be able to handle. This wasn't negativity. It was genuine concern for both me and the integrity of the department.

"This has been our case for too long to turn it over to someone else; besides I already knew Mules did it. I mean, her heart was gone, but yesterday I saw the report and then he called."

"Called?" Jade was standing again, leaning into the circle. She gasped with disbelief, "You talked to him?"

"Yeah, he has called more and more," Dean interjected. He wasn't going to be the one just listening to a conversation.

Sadly sarcastically, "Callow is his favorite person, you didn't know that?"

"Yes," I began controlling the conversation again.

"He called male spouses of victims to torment them that the heart they just picked up outside their home was the heart of their wife who had just disappeared. Then,
when he realized or maybe knew already that I was present when he called them, he asked for me.

"But here's the kicker. It was when he told me not to let people get to me that I dumbly realized that he had tobe there, watching us. At the first vic crime scene, he knew that scruffy, dippity officer was getting on my nerves."

"Don't forget the pool," Dean reminded me.

"Oh yeah, he called, this time using no scramble device, and told me that I could find the other prisoner who had been with him on the bus in a pool, but there was no pool at the location he gave us."

"Pools and hearts, I doubt y'all ever snag him again." Xavier expressed his uncertainty with his typical negativism.

Dean clapped his hands together in excitement as something came to him.

"Callow, it's not Mules, well at least not the one who uses the scrambler." I could almost see a spotlight on Dean, who immediately became the center of attention.

"How'd you figure?" I asked, knowing that many times Dean has quietly put the pieces together before someone else. Maybe vegetables are good for something.

"First, Mules had no need to use a scrambler. Second when the instrument was used and you asked about the pool, the killer didn't know what you were talking about. I think we have two different cases on our hands, a copycat and Mules."

"So who's the copycat?" Jade asked, trying to get it all out of Dean.

"I don't know, but whoever it is, they have been watching us."

We all were silent, pondering the new information, searching for a meaning to the cacophony that could unwind, making sense out of nonsense.

"I don't pay y'all to sit around." The chief wanted us to be aware of his presence.

"Chief, we are trying to solve two cases..." Dean tried encouraging Chief to leave us to our work.

"Looks to me like my top detectives are lollygaggin'." Chief let the silly sounds slowly roll with light sarcasm that didn't mean much.

"Hey," I was now on my feet walking around the desk to join the others.

"When we arrived at the Guidry body, how many patrol cars you saw?" I asked Dean, deciding not to entertain Chief's indication.

Hearts

"I can only recall seeing one. Why?" Dean asked, confused.

"Yeah, me too," I admitted, as I scythed through the last piece of my theory.

"But what strikes me as odd now is when we were leaving, only the two male officers got into that vehicle and Beales vanished."

"You think she..."

"Yeah. That's exactly what I'm thinking."

"What about a pool?" Xavier asked about the new information for him, reminding us we have two cases.

"What pool? A swimming pool?" Chief was very interested and was trying to make sense of the few pieces of the large puzzle that he had no idea where they went.

"The pool the inmate who was chained to Mules is supposed to be in," Jade quickly clued him in.

"Yeah, we know he's in a pool, but he gave us the wrong address."

"No, he gave us the wrong street."

Finally it made sense to me. "Remember where we found him the first time."

"He was working out of that abandoned house," Dean remembered.

"And it had a pool--it was empty!"

"Well what are you two waiting for?" Chief asked, rushing us out the door. "Go bust him."

Perry E. Zenon

Chapter 11

The streets of the French Quarter buzzed with activity as voices, music, laughter, and excitement flooded the jazzed atmosphere.

Jamie Beales, wearing stylish boots that were unusual for her, crisply walked her way through the crowd of people down Bourbon Street, looking for something. Her mousey brown-blonde hair was loose, just past her shoulders; her brown eyes and full crimson lips could have encouraged any man and some women.

She passed by a strip club featuring a sign that read "boys will be girls" and she crossed the street, going into a bar that suited her sexuality better.

Perry E. Zenon

"That's the best damn band there be--ever, Cotton Mouth Kings..." he raised his voice to be heard over the music.

The man was sitting at the bar talking to the bartender.

"You don't know them?" The bartender watched the drunk have the rest of his beer, and talking loudly to him over the smooth music, "Where you been, man?"

"What'll you have?" the bartender asked, relieved to move to the red-lipped woman from the drunken conversations of the guy who didn't know jazz.

"Glacier Bay," Jamie ordered and reached into her pocket for money.

Finding what she was looking for, Jamie took her drink and left the bar in search of greener pastures.

"Hey, you show me something and I'll give you these."

On the balcony stood a couple of men targeting women, trying to coax them into raising their shirts for strands of cheap, neon-colored, plastic beads that they were dangling over the railing.

A group of pedestrians gathered around a man who was spray-painted gold. He stood as if he were a statue. Jamie placed a dollar into his hand at which point, moving like a robot, he animatedly tipped his hat, did a little dance, and placed the bill in the hat with the others.

His audience cheered and Jamie walked away.

Spotting what she was looking for, Jamie walked towards Canal Street inconspicuously following behind a red head while trying to hear her conversation over the noise of the quarters.

Hearts

When she was almost to the end of the street, and coming to the intersection of Bourbon and Canal, Jamie stopped when she saw a familiar car. She rapidly turned around when she recognized the driver.

*****

On our way to the abandoned house that should still have a pool, Dean and I headed away from the river, down Canal Street. We were hoping to arrive before convict Mitch Bryant drowned.

Two cars behind us followed Jade and Xavier who, Chief Pitre insisted, back us up to ensure Mules wouldn't escape again. I gazed out the window, watching the pedestrians cross the street ahead of us waiting for the light to turn green.

"Hey, look at that," Dean pointed towards Bourbon Street, "there's Officer Beales."

As I glanced over, I saw her face and her stunned crimson lips followed as she turned around to walk faster. I threw the car in park and ran to the car behind us.

"We spotted Beales, go to the pool," I rapidly shouted through the window before running to catch up with Dean who was already after Beales.

Although not as crowded as on a Fat Tuesday, Bourbon Street thickly crawled with enough drunks to make passing through nearly impossible.

I saw my partner standing in front of a bar, glancing around. I ran to him, fearing he lost sight of her. I was perceptive.

Perry E. Zenon

"I don't know where she went," Dean admitted as I came up behind him.

I surveyed the area and saw her on the edge, pushing through the crowd. I took off in a sprint, yanking on Dean to follow me. I decided against trying to run through the middle of the street and jumped onto the sidewalk, returning back to the street when I found the sidewalk to have more obstacles to dodge.

"Watch it," a staggering man shouted as I pushed my way around him.

"Watch out!" Dean warned, and I barely had time to dodge a bottle coming my way.

Beales turned the corner down a side street and I jumped over a bench onto the sidewalk again, trying to shorten the distance between us, and heard Dean, stopped when incorrectly jumping over the bench too. He was in the background yelling, "Go, go, go!"

She took another side street when I rounded the corner, as I vaguely wondered why the department thought it was a good idea we wear unathletic business suits.

*****

When the unmarked car driven by our backup detectives pulled up in front of the abandoned house, Mules went to the rear of the house and peered out of a window, waiting for the two detectives to come around to the pool. He didn't think it would take them this long to figure out that he was at the same place they caught

Hearts

him the first time. His cleverness knew no bounds, though, he realized.

Mules heard the gate creaking as it was pushed open. He pressed himself against the wall so that he would not be seen as they passed by. A shadow was cast in the house followed by a second one, and Mules slowly crept to the door, peeking. He became irate when he did not see Detectives Callow and Dean.

"So," Mules angrily queried as he walked out the house with a nine millimeter aimed at Jade. "I guess I'm no longer on Callow's high priority list."

"Hey, get me out of here," Mitch was able to muster from the inside as the water level rose to his mouth.

"So is this what you have reduced yourself to, drowning pathetic inmates in pools?" Jade accusingly turned around to face pale, yellowish hued, tired looking Mules who was still the color of a convict.

"You have no idea what my life is like." Mules walked closer to the pair. "I was a visionary when the media called me a madman. I made those women pay for their sins when y'all accuse me of taking innocent lives."

"What about your sins?" Xavier retorted. "Who will make you pay for your sins? Who gave you a right to decide how they should pay? You're not God; you're an outraged surgery geek. You're nothing more than a postal worker who was too postal to get hired in the first place."

"Don't play the role of the heroic and become another name on my list," Mules warned, pointing the gun in Xavier's direction. "First, we can watch that one drown, and then we will see if I can motivate Callow to come to ascertain if it's your life that is in jeopardy."

The more the water rose, the faster Mitch expended energy while writhing to get loose. He was facing death, beyond panic, wasting vigor, trying to mutter obscenities that were swallowed in a gargle of the water entering his mouth.

*****

As I came to the corner, I saw a door close and took a chance. It had closed behind Beales. Pushing open the old, decorative door, I could see inside to the kitchen, and its occupants, with a look of dismay, pointed through a swinging door that was swinging closed.

"Sorry," I apologized as I exited through the appointed door.

I decided that she had not gone through the restaurant because there was no commotion in that direction. Instead, I exited from the side door. Success! I saw her at the edge of the building.

She clumsily ran in her boots along the side of the building when I came to where she once stood. I had lost her.

"Callow."

I could barely hear Dean calling my name and I shouted back with quick directions, hoping he could follow my voice. I walked down the alley that had no outlet, where she should be.

Hearts

"I told you we weren't going to be able to do this," Xavier whined to Jade. "We should have left the other two dummies worry about this perp."

"Cain, I don't know why you wanted to be a detective or on the department. You are a whiner; you lack manly parts. You believe that you never can do anything," Jade airily retorted, turning her back to Mules, apparently both embarrassed and out of patience.

"Can you believe her?" Xavier slowly walked over to Mules, engaging him, ignoring his 9 mm threat.

"Women always think they know your problem." Xavier jerked his head, indicating Jade.

The second Mules diverted his attention towards Jade, Xavier reached long, knocked the gun out of Mules' hand and it slid away from him. Attuned to her partner's diversions, Jade was already jumping into the pool after Mitch.

Mules' feeble appearance gave an impression of his modified strength. But Xavier realized he was still possessed with plenty of energy when Mules rammed him against the wall of the house. Xavier fell to the floor and grabbed Mules' foot when he went for his weapon. Xavier abruptly pulled Mules to the ground.

Jade worked against extremely limited time freeing Mitch, using her knife, the chair for leverage and strength. Once released, Mitch didn't even look her way as he energetically and frantically dog paddled to the edge. With plenty of adrenaline to spare, Mitch surfaced for good and had he realized he was still an escapee he wouldn't have stayed around.

Xavier struggled to his feet, attempting to get to Mules again before he reached the gun. Mules beat, grabbed the gun, rolled over as he fired at Xavier and hit him in the chest before fleeing out of the gate. Jade was helpless to draw her wet firearm and powerlessly watched the gate as it closed behind him.

*****

I tried to listen for any movement of Beales and could hear nothing but sweet jazz music with a coronet lead from the next street. There were two dumpsters to the right and I walked toward them, aware that she was trapped nearby.

I came to the first, peered inside to make sure she wasn't lying with the trash. When satisfied, I headed to bin number two.

I wasn't prepared for her to race at me from behind. She must have hidden behind the Dumpster. I was suddenly attuned to every sound and movement and heard her footsteps intensifying. I turned, automatically bringing my service weapon into position. She used a board like a bat to violently knock it out of my hand. The same movement connected with my head as if it were the ball.

"This is the thanks I get?" Indignantly, Beales tossed the board behind the Dumpster and raged.

Hearts

"She didn't deserve you, you were good to her, but that wasn't good enough to keep her from cheating on you, why are men so stupid?"

"Callow, hey bro." Dean's voice was a little clearer now.

My vision continued to be a blur, and I failed to remain conscious as I crumbled the rest of the way to the asphalt.

Perry E. Zenon

Chapter 12

I sensed my head pulsating and I opened my eyes to see Dean kneeling over me. I could no longer hear the music from the clubs in the area and wondered how long I had been lying here.

I looked at Dean to inquire about the time and realized he was talking because I could see his mouth moving. Then it dawned on me. It wasn't that they stopped playing; my hearing and vision were foggy. Then, his person and words were back into focus.

"What were you saying?"

"I said this is no time for you to be taking a nap. Are you done now, Detective Sleeping Beauty?"

"Just help me up, would ya?"

Perry E. Zenon

"Where did she go?" Dean inquired, while extending his hand and wrist for me to grab in a climber's secure hold.

"I'm not sure, she hit me with a board and, uh, here you found me," I replied, rubbing the impact spot.

Dean tried to convince me to get to the hospital but I turned down the plea. He eventually gave up and then switched to jokes.

"I know I told you to give women a chance, but I didn't mean start with her," Dean joked. "On a serious note, Jade is at the hospital with Xavier and Mules got away."

"Hospital, what happened?" I asked, forgetting they'd gone to the abandoned house ahead of us.

"Jade said Cain was shot."

"We have to go," I woozily insisted.

Dean was firm. "No, we don't have to do anything. I can handle it. Besides, you have to go home to my godchild. I will walk on over to Charity and if I need you I'll call. Get some rest. I'll see ya' in the morning."

*****

I turned off the car and placed my head on the steering wheel with eyes closed, concentrating on stopping my head from throbbing. I opened the door, leaving my paperwork in the passenger's seat for me to collect in the morning, while wishing I could leave my aching head with it. I reluctantly carried it with me inside.

"How was work, Daddy?"

Hearts

Eve-Marie was sitting in the living room listlessly reading an algebra book, sort of cramming for a final exam. The stereo was playing one of her CDs.

She often tells me I'm too old to appreciate the music, but I'm sure it's just that my head doesn't stop reverberating long enough to listen well. I have stared at the cover's yellow cartoon boy with spiked hair, trying to understand the joy she finds in the musical family with odd hairstyles.

"It was work," I wearily responded, sitting down but wanting to collapse onto the sofa.

"How's school? Mrs. Cruz gave you a last-minute assignment?"

"No it's this algebra, I just don't understand it. It keeps slipping away from me and I only have a week to get it right for the exam," Eve-Marie admitted.

I motioned, she handed the book to me, and I turned it right side up toward me and glanced at the problem she was working on.

"Okay," I began moving closer so both of us could see the book, "What seems to be the problem?"

"The problem is," she hadn't looked up, "these two guys decided to sell lemonade, and now they want me to figure out how many stupid cups of each size they sold." Eve-Marie, my caramel beauty, sounded disgusted. And she sounded her age.

I read over the problem she was working on to get a better understanding.

"They sold twenty-five of the large cup and twenty-two of the smaller one," I reiterated to her and leaned back in the sofa, relishing in the fact that I still had what it took for ninth grade math.

"How can you just look at it and come up with the answer like that?"

The last time I helped Eve-Marie with her homework, she concluded that she wasn't smart because she didn't catch on as quickly as I did. Competitive little thing.

"I remembered this one from a similar one I had to do in school. They always have kids selling weird containers of lemonade," I said. Although I didn't really remember a similar problem, it was only partially false `cause I'm sure I did one. Everyone had to at one point.

Eve-Marie looked over her shoulder at me and I could tell that she was skeptical of my reason, and she noticed my disheveled state wordlessly. I went into the kitchen to see if she had already cooked something. Then I opened the pantry to see what was available to cook.

"This one is harder then the first one," Eve-Marie expressed, opening the door for more quality interaction.

"Let me see," I requested, walking back into the living room.

I read, "Six people in a club will share the expenses of a party that cost two-hundred and forty dollars. How much will Katie pay for her share of the party if the club owes her eight dollars?"

I realized she was in need of a break from her homework. I wasn't in the mood to cook and decided to use this condition as an excuse to eat fast food.

"I don't get it," she complained and petulantly tossed her pencil into the book.

Hearts

"Me either," I lied to keep her from feeling like she was the only one who didn't understand.

"What you say we go get something to eat and tackle this on a full stomach?" I figured it helped at work; it could definitely help here too. People seem to really bond over food too.

*****

We, the two people who claimed we didn't care where we ate, took thirty minutes to decide on a particular place. Eve-Marie and I took an additional fifteen in the car changing directions every time we changed our minds.

I decided to make a parental decision and turned into the parking lot of the only place not on the list of places we didn't want to eat.

We walked up to the window and were teased by the grilled burgers, fries, and onion rings we smelled when the cashier opened the sliding window.

"Welcome, can I take your order?" the teen asked from the other side of the walk-up window.

"What do you want, honey?" I asked Eve-Marie for I was in another indecisive mood.

"I want the number four with a strawberry milkshake."

"That sounds good. I'll take that too, but with a light soft drink." I had to have some virtue about my intake. I always eat very buttered popcorn at movies, but diminish calories by adding diet drinks.

Perry E. Zenon

"Daddy, what happened to your head?" Eve-Marie gasped, noticing the discolored bruise that was turning uglier.

"What this little scratch represents," although I never lie to her I try to make my job seem less of a health risk, I modify the danger. "Some dippity woman wasn't ready to go to jail yet." I controlled my vocabulary admirably.

We took our sack of cholesterol over to the umbrella table where we could divvy the contents amongst ourselves and consume the nutrients.

Eve-Marie bowed her head to bless her food with the sign of the cross, and when she lifted her head she realized I still didn't do the same. Once again, I was already eating my food.

"Dad."

"Yes, love."

"Why don't you say your blessings anymore?"

Since my wife's death, I slowly deteriorated spiritually and blamed God for taking her away from me. I felt she died as a result of something I had done. My overwhelming guilt had led me to a life of quasi-solitude, unwilling to be alleviated of the responsibility for the death of the wife I had been blessed with.

"Because I fear that if I start any conversation with Him, it will turn into me yelling at Him."

I grabbed another fry and took the wrapper off my burger, ready to be on a different subject though I knew Eve-Marie wouldn't settle for an answer without an explanation of the reply.

"Why do you want to yell?"

Hearts

"I don't want to yell, I just know that it will turn out that way because that's what we do when we are mad at someone."

I was really wishing she would let it go.

"Why are you mad at God, Daddy?"

Grimly, "Because He took your mother away."

I couldn't suppress tears and walked back to the window for ketchup, although she knows I don't eat ketchup, but it gave me time to compose myself for her sake; I lied.

"They never put ketchup in the bag." I choked as I tossed the packets on the table and sat down.

"Daddy," she persisted, "God didn't promise it was going to be easy, but He did say He would see you through it."

I studied a car coming through the drive-thru and mulled over her statement, remaining silent. I started to realize there was truth in that simple innocence.

Sometimes I stare at nature when I need to space out and think. As I stared into the sky tonight, it's times like this when I regret not moving to the simplicity of the country that holds all of the stars.

"What you say about us moving to the country?"

"Da-a-ddy. You always do that."

"Do what, I'm just..."

"You change the subject," her voice quavered with sadness and anger. "Why can't you just face the fact that Mom's gone and it's not your fault, it's no one's fault." She was very firm as tears gently rolled down her face and I joined her.

Perry E. Zenon

"I just want you to be happy, that's all. I want it to be like it was, when Mom was alive."

I held her silently and closely, comforting us both. We didn't finish our not-so-healthy meal anyway before heading home, feeling satiated with our loving relationship.

*****

I opened the door, and everything was as we left it. I remembered the algebra problem we left off on. I placed my keys on the wall mount and sat on the sofa, taking up the remote and began to scroll through the channels.

"Thirty-two." I announced this as she sat in front of her books again.

"What?" She was puzzled.

"I didn't want you to think that I conveniently forgot I was helping you with your homework. The answer to your last problem is thirty-two."

She stared at the book and I was not sure whether she didn't believe me or if she was trying to understand for herself how I reached the answer.

"You understand why that's the answer?" I asked this after going through all of the channels, still scrolling with the mute on.

"First you take into consideration that if the bill is two hundred and forty dollars and six people are splitting the bill, then each share is forty dollars."

I placed the remote on the coffee table, settling for the Discovery Channel.

"Yeah, but you said thirty-two, not forty, Dad."

Hearts

"You have to minus the eight the club owes Katie," I reminded her.

"Oh yeah!" She exclaimed and wrote in the final answer. "You knew that the whole time, didn't you?" she asked over her shoulder.

I shook my head indicating yes.

Spontaneously, "I love you, Daddy."

"I love you too, my Caramel Elf."

I sat back on the sofa, watching a caterpillar crawling on the ground while unaware that a spider was stalking him, waiting for the opportune moment to strike. My eyelids became so heavy and the room gave up and got dark.

*****

"Jack."

I struggled to open my eyes as I heard my name and started looking for the source of the familiar voice.

"God is not to blame for your loss."

Standing before me was a perfect, chocolate-colored woman in a soft peach dress. I began sobbing as I gazed upon my wife's face for the second time in eighteen months.

"You cannot continue to hold a grudge against God for the cruelties of the world." Her voice was softer than the morning breeze.

"You drain yourself of viable energy when it is used up in pain and anger.

"God did not take me away from you. As you have learned, that was the work of someone else, a human person, not God."

I had so many questions I wanted to ask but it seemed as though I wasn't required to put voice to them.

"There's no excuse for what I did and that's in the past now. Don't let a life physically lost keep you from living. Eve-Marie has learned from you for thirteen years, but now it's time for you to learn from her. You know that God loves you, and He sends the innocent to teach us."

My eyes peacefully closed. I was ready to be in harmony.

Wednesday

Precious in the sight of the Lord
Is the death of his Saints.

Psalms 116:15

Perry E. Zenon

Chapter 13

My eyes opened; the crawly spider was gone. My
television program was no longer on the Discovery
Channel. Instead, it now featured a cartoon boy with a
football head. My sense of smell also became activated
as I caught a whiff of the morning breakfast pick-me-up.

"Daddy, you're going to be late for work," Eve-
Marie informed me, suggesting I get into the shower to
begin the day.

"Good morning, hun," I greeted her as I rose from the
sofa and stretched. "Can you please make me a cup of
cappuccino?"

"We don't have any more." Eve-Marie walked over
to the cupboard and opened the door so she could look
inside. She next went to the refrigerator.

Perry E. Zenon

"So, do you want coffee, milk, water, or juice? We have grape and apple."

I stiffly arose from the swayed impression I'd made from my all-night sleep, walked around the sofa, and headed down the hall to the back of the house where the rooms were.

"I'll have some apple, thank you kindly."

I entered my room. Blissfully, my suit was already laid on the bed. This time I held onto my whispered appreciation to Heather, telling myself that saying thank you wouldn't bring her back. Reality says that my daughter is the one I should thank, should have been thanking for all the years since my wife's death.

Why can't you just face the fact that Mom's gone and it's not your fault, it's no one's fault.

I entered my bathroom with my daughter's important, life-changing words echoing through my mind. I brooded over their implication as I prepared for the day ahead. I began to weigh my cowardly withdrawal from living against taking the risk.

Once refreshed, dressed, and ready to go, I went into the kitchen where Eve-Marie already had the food on the table and was pragmatically sitting down eating.

"Thank you for getting my suit for me." Eve-Marie looked up from her plate and bewilderedly looked at me. "You don't have to try and do so much."

I sat in my favorite chair and took a big whiff of the food that lay in wait on the plate before me.

"This smells good; you've outdone yourself, Elf."

Hearts

I picked up my fork, poking a piece of egg. I gently released the fork, realizing I hadn't given thanks, and I crossed myself and bowed my head to say my blessing.

Eve-Marie waited for me to raise my head. "Who are you and why are you wearing my father's clothes?" She really was an elf.

I smiled at her indication that I had to be someone else.

"Hey," I gestured with my fork, "just because you're thirteen doesn't mean you can't be right."

"Me," she pointed to herself with her fork. "I'm right? This coming from the man who once told me that he was right because he was my father."

"That's because you were only ten and at the time, and I distinctly remember that I was right."

We laughed at ourselves and ate the rest of our food before it could get too cold and rushed out the door to keep either one of us from being late.

I pulled in front of the school and turned towards her, expecting my hug before she left. Instead, she gazed at me and I could see a deep sense of worry in her eyes.

"Dad," she began as she lowered her gaze to her hands. "I need you to promise me something."

"What's that?" I replied with an eagerness to calm her worried heart.

"Promise me that you will ask God for guidance before chasing a dippity woman with a board again."

"I promise." I laughed only because I instantly pictured me running foolishly after a scraggly woman brandishing a huge board, with determination to use it.

Perry E. Zenon

"I mean it! I can't lose you too because of your stubbornness. And when you do ask, be prepared to react when He responds, because He will."

After promising to ask God for help, we parted at her school. I went into work expecting another hideous package and was relieved when I cleanly made it to my desk. Dean came up to me in the hall to give me an update on current affairs before grappling with the issue of Beales and her heart boxes.

"What's her name?" I teased Dean, noticing the fact that he hadn't stopped smiling since I walked in the door.

"Who?"

I teasingly confronted my partner, "I assumed you met some dame since you're smiling so much. You got lucky at the hospital or something?" Although my head still ached, the change in my body and soul was preparing me for a lighter outlook.

"No, but I will tell you what I have done." Dean began. "I did a search for her name in the database."

"OK, now it's my turn to ask you who."

I indicated I wasn't aware to whom he was referring.

"Here." Dean handed me a printout that had begun his methodical search.

"We have thirty-six adults with the last name Beales in our system, but not one has the first name Jamie."

"Maybe it's not her real name." I didn't put anything past her; with every new criminal came a new set of possibilities to eliminate.

Hearts

"Speaking of names," Dean pulled a piece of paper out of his pocket, "this was on the ground when I found you last night."

In his hand, Dean held a torn peace of notebook paper with the name Nancy Perez written on it.

"That's not mine." I was surprised.

"I knew you were going to say that." He placed the scrap squarely on the desk. "This is why I ran a search for this name as well."

Dean's anal thoroughness could always be relied upon when it came down to finding a lead. If I thought back far enough, I could probably credit every breakthrough, one way or another, to Detective Dean Smith.

He handed me another printout. "I think we should start with this one."

I looked over the paper to see what he was indicating.

"There's only one on the paper," I noted.

Patiently, "I know."

"So what're we waitin' on?"

"I know how you like to feel as though you are the decision maker, so I was just waitin' on you to decide on agreein' with me."

*****

The humidity had dropped to the sixties, made the still, breezeless temperature feel stifling.

She strolled aimlessly along the street as the sun drained her body and caused her face to be visibly beaded with sweat. Jamie turned right off the sidewalk, taking the cobblestone path up to the stucco house and headed toward the friendly front door. No one should be home at this time of the day so, assuming that the front door would be locked, she veered off the path, taking another leading to a gate that accessed the rear of the house.

Next to the house sat a garbage can with the lid halfway off. She first heard an angry buzzing sound and then could see fat, white maggots moving about over themselves inside the can, even spilling out. Repulsed, she moved as far away as she could to ensure none of the little potential flies attached themselves to her or to her clothing.

The back door was locked. Jamie returned to the front, looking around for a key she was sure would be hidden. As her first good luck for several hours emerged, she triumphantly found it stashed in the flower pot.

When Jamie Beales opened the door, she immediately felt the cool air as it pushed past her, escaping the house. The front door entered into a living room badly in need of an interior decorator.

To the left of the door was a staircase leading to the second floor. Straight ahead was a hall which led to what could be a dining room that had two closed pocket doors, badly needing revarnishing.

Jamie carefully closed the door behind her, making sure no unnecessary noises were made to alert anyone who might be in the house. Jamie, listening intently, stood in the living room trying to determine if anyone else was in the house. Once convinced she was alone,

Hearts

Jamie went down the hall and, being more assertive, opened the door to the garage.

Perry E. Zenon

Hearts

Chapter 14

Dean persistently called the home number listed for Nancy Perez. Receiving no answer, we hoped we were not too late. Turning the corner onto the street where the house was located, we approached the house. A car pulled into the driveway of the residence. We pulled behind it and quickly got out.

"Mrs., you can't go inside." Coming around from the passenger side, Dean showed his badge and issued the warning to the bottle-enhanced redhead before I had a chance to get a word out.

"What you mean? This is my house, how you goin' to tell me I can't go into my own house?"

"Mrs. Perez." She stopped and stared at me. "We received a call that someone was entering your house.

So will you allow us to check first to make sure no one is there?"

"You mean someone might be in there right now?" Nancy asked this with wonder, sounding as though she wasn't aware that criminals existed in today's neighborhoods.

"It's a possibility," Dean responded in his usual dry, sarcastic way, but she didn't know it.

"Well by all means, check the house, and don't forget the closets either." So she was pretty savvy after all.

We opened the door using her key and went straight into the living room. We split up, Dean checking the upstairs level while I checked the first floor. We checked every possible space someone could hide. I opened a door, expecting to find another closet, instead finding the garage.

The four windows in the garage door were painted garish orange, allowing only little beams of light to shine through the spots that were not painted. I earched the wall for a light switch. Unable to locate one, I slowly descended the steps into the dark.

"What are you doing?" I turned around to see Dean standing at the door looking down at me from the top of the few stairs.

"Why didn't you just turn on the lights?" Dean flipped a switch outside the door and the garage was illuminated.

The garage was converted into a work area, with power tools, rotary saws, wrenches, and drills. Mr. Perez could probably make anything out of wood.

Hearts

"Well, I haven't found her. What about you?" I asked Dean as I turned around to go back up the stairs.

"Oh, gosh, I forgot to tell you. I saw her upstairs but came back down to see what you were doing instead of placing her under arrest."

"OK, smart ass, let's be gone."

We walked outside and Nancy Perez was standing anxiously on the porch, with the sun shining on her hair in a slightly red glow.

"Well, did you get him?"

"No, it probably was a false alarm, sorry to have bothered you."

We got into the car and, after pulling out of the driveway, left the neighborhood.

"Now what's our game plan?" Dean questioned me from the passenger's seat.

"I don't know, but she's not there."

"Who's to say she won't be later?" Dean insisted. "We can't just leave. Mrs. Perez is in danger."

I made the next right as I tried to figure out what we needed to do.

"So what are we going to do, ask her if we can come in and have a cup of tea?"

"Tea," Dean looked at me, grossly puzzled. "What do I look like to you, some bloody tea sippin', Black English Lord?"

"Well, with your extensive, mysterious background, I'm sure you have English blood in you somewhere."

"I saw a for sale sign in front of a house on the other side of the street." He ignored my frivolity.

Perry E. Zenon

"You want us to go look at a house for sale while this lady is going to go through heart surgery?" I asked Dean, not understanding and not finding that idea pleasing.

"No, Callow, we can just park there and wait to see if she shows up," he patiently responded.

"Good idea. I see we now have a handle on it."

We came around the corner again and I pulled into the driveway of the house that was for sale. I called the precinct to let the chief know that we had followed a lead to Nancy Perez's address. I gave him the address and told him we were watching to see if Jamie Beales showed up.

"Hey look." Dean tapped me and pointed to the Perezes' house. "She's going over to the neighbor's."

This wasn't exactly expected. But I rolled with the surprise. Then I closed my eyes, remembering my promise to Eve-Marie, and asked God to forgive me for the way I had been acting and to guide me today and the rest of my life. I ended the prayer with a ritualistic but meaningful sign of the cross.

I opened my eyes.

"Did that board knock some sense into you or something?" Dean inquired, quietly amazed.

"No, the only thing that board did was give me a headache, but who knows what its purpose was," I responded thoughtfully.

"Well, whatever is responsible for you talking to the Lord is significant and beautiful. I know I sure couldn't get you back where you needed to be in order to recapture having a life."

Hearts

"That would be your godchild, and yes, she's more than great. Frankly, the seeds you planted were very effective too, bro'."

I opened my door, feeling prompted to move.

"Let's go."

As I stood up, I saw Nancy Perez going around to the back of the house.

Perry E. Zenon

Chapter 15

Jamie peered through the filthy curtain and watched as her target walked onto the porch from the side of the house, a direct path from her home next door. Jamie waited inside, standing at the window with a rag in her hand.

Oblivious that she was being watched, Nancy rang the doorbell. When no one answered, she began to look through the plant pots for the key that usually was left there for her.

Jamie checked her pockets and realized that she hadn't placed the key back in the pot. As she contemplated a way to get to Nancy, she heard the opening gate creak.

Uncertain as to what Nancy was doing, Jamie walked to the back of the house. She watched the shadow of Nancy pass by the windows as the latter perambulated toward the rear of the house. As Nancy passed by the kitchen window, Jamie figured that Nancy went to the back door to see if she could gain entry from there.

Cleverly, Jamie carefully released the lock and stood in wait behind the door.

Jamie excitedly prepared for what she knew was going to take place: first dousing the rag with chloroform, and then visualizing cutting her heart out.

The doorknob turned.

The door opened inward and Jamie stood absolutely still to not give away her position. Nancy entered the kitchen. As she walked toward the familiar living room, Jamie marched behind her.

"Oh, you scared me," Nancy was startled and clutched her breast. "No one answered so I thought no one was home. He told me to just use the spare to let myself in if I ever needed to borrow anything."

She was rattling, on the defensive when she should have been challenging the intruder.

"You take me for a fool," Jamie spat, holding the rag down to her side.

"Oh no, not at all." Nancy was frantically trying to accommodate and looked puzzled. "Why would I think that?"

"You must, if you think I don't know you're doin' him when I'm not home. Your husband doesn't deserve

Hearts

this, but he does deserve your black heart. I'll make sure he gets it." Jamie was ferociously spitting words of venom.

As the perpetrator advanced, Nancy, frightened, backed away, trying to keep distance between the two of them. So this was the wife? What? Jealous? She hadn't known.

She finally turned to run but failed to also back away quickly enough. Jamie reached forward to grab Nancy's hair, which streamed out at an angle when she turned. Jamie was able to get a good hold on it. She yanked, pulling her victim back. Then she shoved the rag over Nancy's nose and mouth.

*****

We had seen Perez walking around to the rear of the house so we went after her. Dean and I crept alongside of the house, steering clear of the overrun-by-maggots garbage can while trying to not make any noise.

After our earlier encounter with the woman when she thought we'd made a mistake, we wanted to make more certain that we were right. If we played cowboy, charging back there brandishing guns and badges, we could find Nancy Perez feeding the neighbor's dog for them while they were gone.

We came to the same corner as Nancy when she walked into the house and left the door open. We walked over to it so we could get a better visual.

As we gained a sense of the inside of the house, I saw the back of a woman who I realized was Beales. She grabbed Nancy's enhanced red hair. Before I could draw my weapon, she'd placed a rag over the vic's face and Mrs. Perez's body unceremoniously hit the floor before we were inside.

Yelling with drawn weapons, "Police, don't..."

Before I could finish the sentence, Jamie went through the door out of the kitchen as Dean and I rushed into the house, closing the door behind us.

"She ran yesterday, what made you think she was going to stay today?" Dean asked, not joking.

I watched the door Jamie exited from while Dean stooped down, checking to make sure Nancy was conscious. Then, with a nod, he indicated that she had a pulse.

"Well, I figure if I can have a change of heart overnight, who's to say she can't?"

Talking about hearts and all, "Why don't you go ask her what she has?"

"Where's your board now?" I called out to her with bravado although I really was nervous about walking through that door and giving her another swing at me.

"Hey, you want to come give us a hand with Nancy?" Dean yelled to her in the air as he walked to the door, showing no fear of a board to the head.

Dean began walking out of the kitchen, briefly saw a movement out of the corner of his eye, and as if he were a boxer dodging a right hook, he used his agility to move away from the archway in time to avoid a vase crashing against the wall where his head once was. Looking at the splattered vase and then at each other, we decided we needed to take another plan of action before we lost our heads.

I heard the steps creak as Jamie ascended and Dean went through the door once more, with me bringing up the rear. The living room was decorated in various shades of green with dark brown tables and entertainment center.

"I guess they like green," Dean factitiously suggested as he began to take the stairs.

I couldn't believe it. I heard another vase break as it came in contact with his head and saw Dean fall against the wall.

"Don't worry about me, get Jamie," Dean mustered as I came to his side to see if he was all right. He slipped into unconsciousness.

The flight of stairs in this old home seemed longer than a normal staircase and I climbed slowly, watching for Jamie while anticipating a vase being flung in my direction at any time.

I stood at the beginning of a hallway that held five doors with the grand prize behind one of them. I had reached the top without having to dodge pottery.

I heard the front door open and I headed back downstairs. I heard the door opening and Dean was unconscious.

I expected the entering male owner to be freaked upon seeing two bodies lying unconscious in his house, particularly if his mind may be set upon a quickie waiting for him.

Perry E. Zenon

Chapter 16

A person, not even a cop, would not expect to see an unconscious man lying at the foot of his stairs when he entered his home during his lunch break.

Strangely, the man of the house simply closed the door behind him, not seeming to find it out of place that Dean was sprawled on the floor.

On the contrary, Larry Mules recognized Dean's face, delighted, figuring that if Dean Smith was here, then Callow wasn't far away.

A step squeaked as someone started down the stairs and Mules reached into the familiar coat closet, grabbed a bat, and stood against the wall, waiting for Callow to come down.

Perry E. Zenon

I slipped around the corner of the enclosed stairs, snuck past Dean, and saw the swinging bat, but it was too late to dodge the highly unexpected impact. I dropped to my knees as my gun uncontrollably fell out of my grasp and thudded onto the floor.

I looked up, staring into the eyes of a man I have despised for years.

"Jamie!" Mules yelled, standing over me with bat in hand. "Get down here and give me a hand."

The stairs creaked as she descended to the bottom level, smirking in admiration for herself and perhaps Mules.

Mules kicked my gun away from me; I rolled onto my back, trying to catch my breath.

"Watch him." Mules demanded, giving her his gun before going into the kitchen and returning with a chair. "Make him sit in this chair," said the man accustomed to taking prison command of the fledglings.

Knowing exactly what lay inside, Mules went to a closet to retrieve two extension cords, using one to bound Dean's hands, came back to the chair, and used the other to tie me to the chair.

"That should hold you until we are ready for you," Mules spat contemptuously, spraying me with wicked spittle.

"I thought you worked separately." I was weak and feeling very confused as he started to walk away.

"Well, we all know cops don't get paid for what they think, so just sit there and try not to talk, because I don't want to hear it."

Mules turned around, looking down on me.

Hearts

"I told you I didn't commit all the murders, but you didn't believe me."

Mules leaned over so that he hissed directly into my ear, "Jamie took the pleasure of killing those adulterous women, like your wife."

Jamie mocked with glee, "It was Larry's idea to kill more than just the unfaithful and we struck an agreement

that I got to kill all those on my list of names." I was offended by the stench of cigarette smoke that clung to her. And, of course, by her presence and measured insanity.

"You do know that there are places for people like you?" I asked, not exactly trying to help but trying to take back some control.

"Places for people like us?" Jamie shot back her retort in rapid fire and I could tell that she didn't find my statement amusing.

"People like us are the ones who ensure the evil are punished."

"Your supremely knowledgeable statement of choice." I couldn't help but mock her stupidity and remembered how it was easy to tire of her. Already.

"God is the only one who can hand down punishment for our sins." I was a bit surprised how my God knowledge came back so rapidly once I had removed the block.

Triumphantly, "Well, well, I have an answer for you. I am so enjoying filling you in before your, uh, demise. Here is the game plan that, I might add, was successfully executed, due to the superiority of the odds being stacked against you. I unilaterally decided to kill them all and let Him sort them out when they got to the being they so helplessly believed in."

Mules was through gloating over me as he took his gun from Jamie and pointed it at my head.

"And I say we send you to your destiny right now."

"No." An excited Jamie pulled Mules' arm down to his side.

Gleefully, with excitement, "I want to finish off Nancy, then I will do him. I've never seen what a righteous heart looks like."

I closed my eyes and began to fully, seriously pray, knowing that if anything could get me out of this situation it would be my heavenly Father.

"You're praying now?" Mules realized when seeing that I closed my eyes. "Oh, you filthy pig, you think God is going to come down from heaven to save your pathetic soul." He was amused and highly patronizing.

I opened my eyes and stared into malevolence.

"What in heaven's name is the world coming to?" Mules ridiculed, relishing his generic religion-related reference. He went up the stairs. "I'm going to change."

After a careful look to assure my bonds were stable, Jamie seized Dean's gun and went to the kitchen to drag Nancy down into the basement where she would complete her latest operation.

I listened to the methodic second hand tick as it worked its way around the clock hanging on the wall. It was grounding that something was orderly.

Dean waited until Mules was upstairs before he crawled over to me with a big, broken piece of the vase that he held behind his back.

Hearts

"He won't be up there long, you might want to move it along," I urged Dean, desperate to be free.

I rose from the chair, taking the wire from around my wrist, and contemplated whether I should go upstairs after Mules or in the basement after Beales, but upon hearing a door close upstairs, decided on neither. I grabbed the bat, trying to breathe shallowly and silently, waiting for him to come down the stairs.

My head had encountered double duty with pain and ensuing confusion within two days. I didn't realize that Mules would notice Dean was no longer at the foot of the stairs. As he turned the corner, I swung the bat with the fervor of the kid who knows this shot will make his potential career. With advance notice to be prepared, the perpetrator easily dodged in time to evade.

He ducked, and with real power behind his force, using his entire body, easily rammed his shoulder into my already sore abdomen, folding me into the wall. I failed to keep a grip on my improvised weapon. The bat plummeted out of my hands.

He swung, catching me off guard, and I dropped back on top of a coffee table that helped to break the impact of my plunge while shattering the ugly furniture.

Remembering the gun's location that I'd been fixated upon, my body rolled to the side. My hand grasped it. I found the familiar trigger and squeezed off two rounds that caught Mules at close range, centered in the chest while he came toward me. His body fell with a quick thud. I could now safely stagger to my feet and observe his lifeless eyes with satisfaction.

Perry E. Zenon

I looked over towards Dean and realized the vase must have caught him good for he had slipped back into his unconscious state. I was going to try to wake him but the disturbance brought Jamie back upstairs from the basement.

I spotted the gun she wielded and I moved behind the wall as she wildly fired with the intent to reunite me with my wife. Then she moved--to someplace.

Hearts

Chapter 17

As my body thinned to hug the wall, I clutched my weapon, poised, waiting for her to make a slip. My sore head was in a newly non-target mode. I visually searched the room for any shiny object that could be used as a mirror to see her movements. Her position was
eluding me.

Scarcely breathing, I quietly listened for movement in or near the kitchen. I heard the ticking of the demon-ic
clock, reminding me of every passing second that my prey wasn't found.

Tick.

Instinct told me it was now or never.

Tick.

Perry E. Zenon

Thoughts flashed in my head. I regretted not putting a bullet in Mules' head instead of his chest for his brutal murder of my Heather.

Tick.

And I could envision myself regretting if I didn't put one in Beales, the scalpel demon who took the liberty to carve to punish the one I cared dearly for.

Tick.

I waited for the second hand to move once more, sounding throughout the house like the starting pistol of a race signaling my time to move. I turned to the right, simultaneously bringing up my weapon, prepared to fire upon the first thing that moved.

The hallway was clear.

I released a sigh, not realizing until then that I seemed to have stopped breathing.

I felt let down because I was eager to end this game and my adrenaline had to redistribute itself. I proceeded to the garage door.

Tick.

I briefly wondered if I was listening to the last seconds of my life get peeled from the orange of existence. But the thought was so brief that I didn't recognize it in my ultimate survival mode. Doing Jamie would result in only the second person I had killed. The last was fifteen minutes ago.

Tick.

I pressed my back against the wall once more.

Tick.

I turned the corner, cautiously looked into the garage, and heard the explosion of a big round as it exited the

Hearts

chamber, simultaneously violently whacking me in the back. Pain shot through my body. Not just pain, but a thunderclap of violent proportions. She was in the kitchen behind me after all. Even with protective armor, the jolt was a good one, designed stronger than the protection.

I whirled around in slow motion to see Jamie standing on the other side of the island in the kitchen before I lost my footing and tumbled down the stairs, hitting the solid concrete basement floor.

Managing to hold on to consciousness, I saw Jamie Beales, with Dean's weapon, at the head of the stairs, aiming straight for the one spot that wasn't protected with armor.

My head.

Tick. Now the clock, my organizer, was in my head.

"Say hello to the adulteress for me when you see her."

Tick.

I was beginning to hate that clock.

Tick.

I thought. The garage echoed with the sound of a round exiting the chamber as I simultaneously wondered

who would take care of my precious Eve-Marie.

Tick.

Nothingness.

Perry E. Zenon

Chapter 18

The crack of the crumbling front door sharply defined the expediency and necessity of kicking it in.

"We got bodies," an officer yelled.

When the neighbors heard gunshots coming from the house, they thankfully, immediately called the police.

Chief was on the radio and was immediately informed about an incident. Realizing the address was near the house his detectives were, he had gone all out, requiring a SWAT response to the call.

The house was a black mass of officers wearing thick, black, bulletproof suits with SWAT on the back in huge yellow lettering. They rapidly searched for the person, or persons, responsible for the bodies strewn in the living room.

"Clear."

They split into two teams as they entered the house. The first team took the stairs up to the second floor, and the second team searched the ground level.

"Clear."

The sound of doors hitting against the wall as they were kicked open jarred the rickety wooden house as the officers searched the few rooms, calling back to the others as each room was cleared of any possible threat.

"House is clear; send in the paramedics."

The paramedics were admitted and the team exited the house, allowing the former to take the medical and coroner targeted shift.

*****

Eve-Marie talked on the phone to her girlfriend about the upcoming party and the invitees. She was sitting on the floor, next to the sofa, semi-watching the television that was mostly there for the comfort of sound.

Her favorite group was singing and hip-hop dancing. Her father would have glanced at them, calling them the Yellow Uglies.

"My dad will be home soon, I have to go." Eve-Marie conscientiously wanted to clean up when she realized the time.

After placing the phone in the cradle, she began cleaning up the small mess she had made in the kitchen before going back to the living room to concentrate on her still weak algebra.

Hearts

Someone gently rapped on the door in diametrically opposite behavior employed in using the sharp, staccato rap the police used when needing to command authority.

"Who is it?" Eve-Marie called cautiously.

Instead of answering her question, the person knocked on the door again.

"Coming."

Eve-Marie went to the door and looked through the peephole but was unable to see who was on the other side.

Sliding the chain in place, Eve-Marie unlocked the door and partially opened it to see outside.

The man stepped more squarely in front of the door where he could be seen as the door was opened, and Eve-Marie became alarmed as she recognized Chief Pitre.

"There's been an accident and your father was shot." Chief Pitre hated this part of his job.

"If you would get your things, please, I will take you to your godfather, Detective Smith. He asked me to gather you and your belongings and bring you to him. He would have come himself, but he has the report to fill out."

She was pretty sure this large man, the grandfather type who wasn't exactly looking her in the eye, wasn't accustomed to delivering heart-wrenching news to a young teen of a fellow officer.

Questions swarmed her mind.

Her body, just like her dad's had, felt as though ice cubes were stuck all over, especially in her throat.

She could only nod.

Perry E. Zenon

She thought of the woman who had chased her father with a board. That wasn't funny.

She gathered some things, including her schoolbooks, and dutifully left with the chief.

Thursday

By This I know that thou favorest
me,
Because mine enemy doth not
triumph over me.

Psalms 41:11

Perry E. Zenon

Chapter 19

She insisted that her godfather, the gentle African-American, large in a comforting way, and now a very sad godfather, take her to see her dad. He knew this is what he must do.

Eve-Marie and Detective Dean Smith held their heads down while standing by her father's side, staring disbelieving at his stillness under the starkly white sheet.

Eve-Marie began to cry.

When she was eleven, she learned about death in the most horrible of ways when her childhood was torn from her by her mother's violent death, and her life changed forever.

She was older now, by almost two years, and had a more pronounced conceptualization of death's finality. Now she was forced to face her father's tranquil body..

Perry E. Zenon

She intellectually understood that life was filled with what the sisters called "trials and tribulations," and sometimes the only thing you could do to overcome the situations you find yourself in, is to leave it to God and let him walk you through it. The concept frustrated both her and Dean when the natural response is to do something and fix the one you love, and concomitantly, your own pain.

Years ago, Dean was designated as the person who would take on the responsibilities of her guardianship and religious upbringing in the event something happened to her mother and father. Today, he stood by her side, never considering faltering in this long-term obligation, one that he considered an honor and a blessing.

It was a week ago Wednesday when the paramedics were called to assist with multiple murders and were startled when Dean grabbed one of their legs as he struggled for breath and consciousness.

*****

The uncanny, bright light stung my eyes as they opened, and I continuously blinked trying to clear my vision of the clouds of white that plagued me.

I closed my eyes tightly, deliberately, not willing to accept where I was in the clouds.

My life was before my eyes and I thought of what I was leaving behind. I wasn't ready to die.

Hearts

"I'm not ready to die," I shouted, opening my eyes, and I realized the white that I saw was from the hospital room I was lying in.

"Daddy!" This came out as a delighted squeal.

I looked toward my feet where Eve-Marie stood and I was comforted to see Dean standing by her side.

"I knew you'd come through."

"What day is it?" I asked through cracked lips.

"Thursday," Eve-Marie was solemn. "Daddy, I love you, I love you!"

"You can't get up." The nurse pushed my chest against the bed. "You need your rest."

"Rest? I've slept a day; don't you think I've slept long enough?"

"No, it's a week later," Jade responded from my side and I was pleasantly amazed she was there.

"After what you've been through you might want to take another week off," Dean joked. When I almost laughed, pain shot through my body.

"Sorry," Dean said. "Please don't laugh. You need your energy. I promise you the future will be full of laughs."

I gently eased into sleep again. When I awoke, Jade was the only one there while the other two were at the hospital cafeteria.

She explained to me that when Jamie Beales was standing in the doorway, Dean mustered his last conscious bit of energy and shot her with his concealed leg weapon, throwing her off balance, and as she fell she fired, hitting me right above the temple.

She also related that Xavier, for whom protective armor worked correctly, was well out of the hospital, and being shot helped his ego, although she factitiously said he might be a little too egotistical now.

She kissed my forehead and I slept better than I had slept in one and a half years.

Friday
(A Year Later)

We give thanks to you,
oh God.
We give thanks.

Psalms 75:1

Perry E. Zenon

Chapter 20

I awoke to the smell of cinnamon and real, brewed cappuccino as the aroma from the kitchen began to waft into the bedroom. Two and a half years ago, my wife would always awaken an hour before me to begin breakfast, while I slept until the sound of the alarm awakened me.

Switching off the new alarm, I smiled, identifying the perfume of the fresh coffee I bought yesterday afternoon at the specialty coffee market, an activity totally out of character in my past. Entering the bathroom, I began my
ritual, making myself better turned-out than when I awoke.

Exiting the bathroom, I was delighted with a glow of warmth when I saw my suit laid out as usual, waiting for me on the bed.

Perry E. Zenon

After stiffly dressing, I stopped by Eve-Marie's room to be her alarm before going into the kitchen. The aroma became more poignant with the added essence of eggs, bacon, and grits that I couldn't smell, but knew were there. I walked behind my exquisite wife and the counter, placed my arms around her, kissing the crown of her head.

"Good morning, my darling."

"Mornin' to you, handsome," Jade replied, turning toward me with two plates in her hand.

"Is she still enjoying her sleeping adaptation?" She was referring to Eve-Marie, who had taken a liking to being a teen.

With the help of Eve-Marie and the Dean Smith support team, I had continued fully coming back to God and because of that I now had a full life.

Twenty-one days after facing down Larry Mules for the last time, God told me it was now the time to let go and move on. Six months later, I happily waited at the end of the aisle as Jade gracefully floated forward to join me in the sanctification of the mass celebrating holy matrimony.

At first, I was naturally concerned about Eve-Marie's reaction when I asked her what she thought about my remarrying. Her role of caregiver was not to be taken lightly and it could be a difficult transition.

I felt enormously relieved when she responded, "I hope you're talking `bout Jade because she's gorgeous...and cool, man."

After the three of us ate together, we dropped the renewed teen at school and headed for work.

Hearts

We arrived just before eight.

"Hey, did you hear?"

Always in the hall at the precise moment we entered, Dean approached with his everyday greeting.

"No, Dean, why would I watch the news and ruin this for you?"

Jade kissed me on the cheek and entered the inner office reserved for homicide detectives. We agreed to not let our personal life interfere with work; I thought Chief would appreciate that, so she left us to it.

"You know Jones from records?" Only Dean knew most of the employees of the building. He was certainly not an elitist who would rather not associate with the non-detectives, as some are.

"I think so, why?"

"He's just missing, that's all. It just seems odd though. Some people think he just can't get past the Samantha girl who was murdered."

We continued walking into the main office, pre-roll call, alive and buzzing and beginning another normal day.

That is, if you consider a double homicide, drowning, and a purposeful, home electrocution to be normal.

©2006 Perry Zenon

Perry E. Zenon

Hearts

For a day in your courts
is better than
a thousand.
I would rather be
a doorkeeper in the
house of my God
Than dwell in the
tents of wickedness.
For the Lord God is
a sun and shield;
He bestows favor and honor.
No good thing does the Lord
with-hold
From those who walk uprightly.
O Lord of hosts,
Blessed is the man who trusts in
thee!

Psalms 84:10-12

Perry E. Zenon

About the Author

   While writing Hearts, Perry E. Zenon served in the United States Army, defending the nation as he moved throughout the world. He finished the book in Germany, where he meet his wife, Moedjirah and her daughter. Perry is the proud father of two daughters, Angel, and Brenna; and son Perry. Although Perry had to move often his place of origin is New Orleans, Louisiana, sometimes the hottest but definitely the loveliest, verdant spot on Earth, where every night the orange sunset touches the water and the crabs leap out, inviting a feast for the city rising in reconstruction. 2006.

   Correspondence for the author should be addressed to:

   Perry E. Zenon
   2669 Highlander Dr
   Gretna, LA 70053

   author@perryezenon.com
   Or the publisher.